Love Shots

Bluestone Series: Book Four

Isobel Reed

Love Shots: Bluestone Series: Book Four
Copyright © 2023 Isobel Reed
All rights reserved.

ISBN: (print) 978-1-958136-60-7
(ebook) 978-1-958136-59-1

Inkspell Publishing
207 Moonglow Circle #101
Murrells Inlet, SC 29576

Cover art by: Fantasia Frog Designs
Edited by: Yezanira Venecia

DEDICATION

For my husband, little bean, and the happily ever after that each day with you brings.

ISOBEL REED

CHAPTER ONE

"What. The. Fuck." Teddy seethed, "I can't believe you just threw a fucking lamp at me!" He could hear his voice getting louder and louder by the second. "What the hell is wrong with you, Summer?"

"*Me?*" Summer's shriek easily matched his volume as her hazel eyes narrowed on him. "What the hell is wrong with *you?*"

A second later, something else was hurtling toward him, only just missing his head. An ear-piercing smash later, he spared a glance at the floor to his left and couldn't help but scowl. This had to be a bad dream. Dark liquid was now seeping into his hardwood floors while crooked shards of glass stood to attention.

"Have you lost your damn mind, woman? That was an eight-hundred-dollar bottle of whiskey!"

"Oh no," she mocked, bringing her chipped red nails up to cup her face. "Sucks when someone takes something that isn't theirs … doesn't it?"

He'd had enough. "For the last goddamn time, Mickey wanted to sell, and I wanted to buy. End of story. You weren't in the country … You're never in the country! How on earth was I supposed to know Mickey promised you the bar? I'm not a damn mind reader, Summer!"

Really, this is all my fault, Teddy thought as he mentally cursed himself. It was too late for this bullshit. Why on earth did he even answer the door? He was old enough and ugly enough to know that nothing good ever came from answering your door after midnight.

He certainly hadn't been prepared to see Summer Willis. Mickey's granddaughter. It had been five long years since he'd seen the beautiful, blonde, pain in his ass. And now here she was, using the contents of his shelf and his living room wall for target practice because, apparently, Mickey had at one point in time offered her the bar Teddy had just purchased.

After muttering some imaginative expletives under her breath, she took a step toward him. Then another. He finally had a chance to study her, something he hadn't been able to do since she'd barged her way into his apartment and started yelling. Something was off. The Summer he knew was always so put together. Composed. Perfect. Even when the words coming out of her pretty little mouth were anything but.

Errant strands of hair hung down from the messy knot at the top of her head. Her short-sleeved blue blouse was slightly crumbled, and he noticed mud stains streaking the knees of her jeans. But it was the skin above the black bracelets covering her wrist that his eyes zeroed in on. Bruises.

What the hell is that?

Before he had time to think, he was reaching for her arm to get a better look. "Who did this to you?" His forceful demand was a direct contradiction to the gentle way he circled her wrist as he held it up.

He didn't miss her flinch. Or the flicker of sadness in her deep green-brown eyes—a rare display of vulnerability there gone so fast … if he'd have blinked, he would have missed it. Her expression had quickly defaulted back to hard as she wrenched her hand back. "None of your business."

Teddy didn't think Summer noticed that she had just basically admitted to a person being responsible for those marks. But he had. And he wouldn't be forgetting any time soon. He wasn't about to push her for more information right now though. Not unless he wanted his apartment trashed even more than it already was.

"What can I do?" He kept his voice calm, even though he was feeling anything but. Someone had hurt Summer. His Summer.

She was never yours.

"Give me back my bar." She retorted.

"You know I can't do that. I know you've not been back for a while, but … ever since I left the Navy, Mickey's has come to mean a lot to me."

Her expression betrayed her again. Instantly going from rage to shock to concern at his revelation. "You left the Navy? Why?"

There she was. There was the woman he remembered. It was good to know she was still there. "Yeah, dollface, I left. Three years ago. Moved back here. Your grandaddy set me up with a job at Mickey's, and now … well, you know the rest."

"Don't think I missed you ignoring the *why*, Teddy." The sass was back.

"That's right, doll. I am ignoring it. Because it's a long damn story, and I'm too damn tired. So, if you're done redecorating my apartment"—he gestured around the small dark room, even more dark since she smashed one of the two lamps that he had—"I think it's time for me to head back to bed."

Summer gulped. How she could look both scary and vulnerable at the same time was a complete mystery.

"I need a job," she blurted. "I planned on working at Mickey's."

A laugh escaped before he had time to swallow it. "Jesus Christ, Summer. This is how you ask me for a job? Barging in here at two A.M., throwing my shit at me, and calling me an asshole?"

The corner of her lips curved up into a smirk. He was reminded right then and there what a smile from Summer Willis could do to him.

"I need somewhere to crash too. I'm assuming that since you're living here, the apartment above the bar is vacant?"

His body was vibrating now. This chick was something else. "You're batshit fucking crazy, you know that?"

A full-blown smile had now blossomed across her face. Her hand went in front of her, palm facing up. "Keys?"

She really wasn't kidding. She wanted him to give her a job and a place to live. After the shit she just pulled. Unbelievable. When he didn't reply quickly enough, she spoke again.

"Come on, Teddy, we both know you're gonna let me stay there. And you know as well as I do, I'm the best darn bartender in this town. I've been working on and off at Mickey's ever since it was legal. Now, hand over the keys and you can go get your precious beauty sleep."

He leaned down, ignoring the vanilla scent filling up his lungs, and whispered into her ear, "Not a fucking chance, dollface."

***

Teddy couldn't sleep. He'd tossed and turned all night after kicking Summer out of his apartment. A mixture of guilt, intrigue, and confusion meant he was now wide awake, and the sun wasn't even up yet. So much for sleeping in.

He stared up at his bedroom ceiling, replaying his fight with her over and over again. What the heck was she doing here? He'd been back in Bluestone three years, and she'd never once ventured back before. Not even for a visit.

One thing was for sure though: Summer Willis had always been his weakness. And if the lack of sleep was anything to go by, she still was. While he was being honest with himself, he should probably also admit that she had been the reason he'd moved back to Bluestone in the first place. Getting a job at Mickey's wasn't a coincidence either. It was a connection to her. The bar her grandfather owned. Well, until recently. Now, Teddy was the proud new owner.

He'd always wondered about her. Even if it had been years since they'd seen each other. Despite them not being on such a friendly basis right now, they had been close at one point in time. Really close. They'd grown up together, and Teddy wasn't ashamed to admit that he'd had one hell of a crush on her. There was even a time he thought she felt the same way about him, but he'd been wrong. Colossally wrong.

Letting out a heavy sigh, Teddy pushed himself up and out of bed. He needed to stop thinking about Summer. That ship had sailed. If he wasn't going to sleep, then he'd do something useful. There was always work to be done at the bar. So, there it was. He had a plan. He would just quickly jump in the shower, then he'd head on over there.

Fifteen minutes later, Teddy was out of the door and headed to Mickey's. What he definitely wasn't doing was thinking about Summer Willis.

Keep telling yourself that, buddy.

Choosing to ignore the troll inside his head, he instead focused on his walk. Living in town had its advantages. He was just a five-minute stroll to the bar. While walking with a purpose through the parking lot, something to the side of him caught his eye. His steps stalled as his attention went to the blue Prius in the far corner. Cursing under his breath, he was back on the move as he started toward it. The closer he got, the angrier he became.

"Un-fucking-believable." He huffed as he came to a halt by the car door.

One knock on the window later, he was looking into Summer's startled eyes. When she didn't immediately roll down the window, he impatiently gestured for her to do so. But she simply frowned and scrunched up her nose. He realized then that his pissed-off expression probably wasn't doing him any favors.

Trying his best to keep his tone gentle, he decided to ask her instead. "Please, Summer, roll down your window."

A cute little grimace took over her face as she pressed down on the window button. "Morning," she shyly greeted.

"You gonna tell me why you're sleeping in your car?"

"Um … I'm being environmentally conscious?"

He raised an eyebrow and was rewarded with a smile that hit him full force in the chest. "You're not staying with Mickey?"

She looked at Teddy like he was certifiable. "Mickey's gone. I thought you knew? He sold the house the same time he sold you the bar."

Teddy had no idea. But that wasn't important right now. What was important was why the hell Summer was sleeping in her car and not staying with friends or in a hotel.

"What about Laney? You couldn't stay with her? Or book into a hotel?"

Running her hand through messy blonde strands, she sighed. "Laney's married and has two kids under five. The last thing she needs is me showing up at her door at two in the morning, asking for a place to crash." He was about to protest but she cut him off. "It's not a big deal, Teddy. Really. It's just one night. You don't have to worry about me bringing down the property prices. Give me a minute and I'll get out of your hair."

"Where will you sleep tonight?"

She shrugged. "I'll find a motel or something."

She'd never been a good liar. She was definitely planning on sleeping in her car again. His gaze drifted to the bags and clothes filling her backseat. She was in trouble, but it didn't make sense. Just a few hours ago she'd been pissed that he'd been the one to buy Mickey's and not her. How could she afford to buy a bar but not a hotel room for the night?

He knew he was seriously going to regret what he was about to say, but he said it anyway. "You can stay in the apartment above the bar. Until you find somewhere." The relief in her eyes twisted his gut. "And I might be able to throw a couple of shifts your way."

Now she was beaming. The guilt he'd been feeling all night came flooding back. He should have given her the keys when she'd asked and saved her from a night in her car. Anything could have happened to her. Anything. And it would have been his fault. All the signs that she'd needed help had been there too. The crumpled, mud-stained clothes, her chipped nail varnish, messy hair.

Some Navy SEAL you are.

Then there was that bruise. His fists clenched at the memory. He knew right then he needed to put his feelings aside and do what he could to help her. Even if she was a giant, beautiful, pain in his ass.

CHAPTER TWO

Five years had apparently been enough time for Summer to forget just how crazy Teddy McCallen made her. He'd always been a moody son of a bitch, that was for sure. A good-looking one at that. But over the years, just like his looks, his broody nature had clearly matured. He was now a ridiculously sexy, six-foot-four ball of rage. And she kind of liked it.

So, so healthy, Summer.

Dropping off the empty glasses she'd collected at the end of the bar, she snuck another look at the man in question. The easy charm he offered each customer was deceptive. If they hung around for just another second, they'd see Teddy's mask drop almost instantly. She saw it though. She'd always seen it. Summer figured that was why he always treated her differently. Although, right about now, she was starting to wish he didn't. She could really go for some of that fake friendly, if it meant that smile was directed her way.

It had been a rough year, but she knew she needed to try and focus on the positive. At least she had a place to stay now. That was something. She would never take for granted hot showers and clean clothes ever again.

Showing up at Teddy's the other night hadn't been her finest hour. She was well aware of what a hot mess she was. But at least now she was a clean, semi-presentable hot mess. And she was determined to try to not piss him off during her first shift at Mickey's.

"Summer. Long time no see." A familiar, deep voice croaked from behind her.

Spinning on her heel, she visibly cringed at the sight. Colton. Her ex. Yet another bad decision she'd made over ten years ago. Great. That was the thing about small towns, exes were always sneaking up on you and reminding you of what a dumbass you used to be.

He looked just as she remembered him. Jet-black hair that was just a little bit too long, piercing dark brown eyes, and enough stubble to be considered the start of a beard. Although he was tall, he'd always been on the lean side. That hadn't changed either.

"Uh, hi, Colt." She smiled and hoped like hell it didn't look as forced as it felt. "How you doing?"

"Doing good, babe. What … no hug?" Colton opened his arms expectantly while she internally screamed.

Fuck my life.

She stepped into his arms and gave him the world's quickest, most awkward hug before retreating back toward the bar counter.

"Well, I better get back to work. It was good seeing you." She spun in the other direction before she'd even finished the sentence. But he didn't let her get very far. She felt his hand wrap around her upper arm, forcing her to a stop, holding her in place. *Goddamnit.* Hadn't she been manhandled enough already? Now she was pissed. Screw being friendly.

"Get your hands off me, Colt. Now." She fumed as she turned to face him.

Luckily, the man was smart enough to drop his hand, but he didn't back away.

"I didn't mean to frighten you, Summer. Come on. It's

me. *Me!* I've done a lot more than grab your arm if I remember correctly, babe." The dirty smirk he gave her made her stomach roil.

Stupid, goddamn small towns.

"I'm not your *babe*, Colt. And I suggest in the future, you don't go around grabbing women in bars unless you're looking for a punch to the throat."

Clearly not too worried about her threat, he took a step closer, crowding her against the bar. "I promise to not go around grabbing women in bars, Summer; I doubt I'm gonna want to now that you're back in town. How 'bout I pick you up after your shift tonight …?" He took a moment to run his eyes over her body. "We can do some catching up?"

Euwww.

"How 'bout you back up before I make good on my promise?"

"Everything all right here?" Teddy boomed from behind the bar. She didn't need to see his face to know it was set to angry.

"Everything's good, Teddy. Summer and I are just catching up. Right, babe?"

Summer was done. She was so sick of men, it wasn't even funny. She shoved Colton's shoulder until he took a step back. Finally. "For the last time, I'm not your *babe*. And don't *ever* touch me again." Chancing a look in Teddy's direction, she was surprised to see just how angry he was. Rage seemed to be seeping out of every pore. Even when she'd thrown a lamp at him, he hadn't looked this pissed. "I'm going on my break."

She didn't wait for an answer. She needed to get out of there.

Her feet didn't stop until she hit the alley next to the bar. Sliding down the brick wall, she winced as her skin met the cobbles, and she wasted no time wrapping her arms around her knees. Tonight probably wasn't the best night to wear shorts, but she couldn't bring herself to care right now. The frigid air was the only thing stopping her from falling apart.

As she dropped her head onto her knees, thoughts of the past year flitted through her mind. Her brain chose that moment to play her an ironic slideshow of all her bad decisions. Perfect. It's not like she needed a reminder. Ben was front and center of the show of course. Even after tonight's display, he could easily swipe the worst ex award right out of Colton's hands.

"You okay?"

Summer startled. She hadn't heard anyone come out or make their way into the alley. Her head shot up and she was even more alarmed to find that Teddy was sitting next to her.

"You scared the shit out of me! How is it, such a big fucker like you, can sneak up on me without making a sound?"

Teddy threw his head back and laughed, which only annoyed her more. Why was he laughing at her?

"A big fucker like me," he said through another throaty laugh, "well, I guess I have the Navy to thank for that."

Summer threw her hands up in exasperation. "Dear Lord, how could I forget? You're a big, badass Navy SEAL." Sarcasm dripped off every word as she rolled her eyes. "They probably have a special class designed just for you. Stealth 101 for big fuckers." She turned back to see him convulsing. "Can you stop laughing at me now?"

"I forgot how funny you are, doll."

She simply glared at him while he got himself under control. But her tension quickly dissipated as she got a good look at his smile. It was aimed her way for once, and it made her feel things. Things she thought she'd buried long ago.

Teddy McCallen was her weakness. Always had been. And apparently always would be. It didn't help that the man was frigging gorgeous. His body was practically a wall of muscle, and even the ink covering both his arms was as sexy as hell. But it wasn't just his dark, messy hair, square jaw, and sparkling green eyes that captured her attention. It was the man himself. The smart, funny, and kind man before her. Sure, he was a little rough around the edges, but he had a heart of pure gold.

He'd practically raised his little sister, Ivy, when his parents passed away. Although he'd been young, and they'd been taken in by their grandparents, Summer had seen first-hand the part he played in raising Ivy. And she would never forget that. He was a good man. Way too good for Summer.

"Seriously, Summer, you okay? If Colton touched you inappropriately, I swear to God I'll rip his throat out."

Her lips twitched. "Harsh."

"Warranted," Teddy countered.

She didn't hold back her smile. "What did I see in him again?"

"Fuck if I know!"

Then she remembered. Colton was supposed to help her move on. Move on from the man she really wanted. The man she'd spent her entire childhood obsessing over. Teddy.

She never dated anyone else before Colton because of her crush. Summer's teenage years were spent waiting for Teddy to realize he was in love with her. But it was in high school when delusion really took over. She actually thought for a while that Teddy liked her back. So what did she do? Flirt with him relentlessly of course. Making a fool out of herself. And breaking her own heart when she realized he'd been sleeping with Becky Matthews the entire time. The perky cheerleader. Talk about clichés.

"I was never any good at choosing men." She sighed, turning away from him and directing her gaze back to her knees.

"No, you weren't." She felt his callused fingers lightly brush her chin as he turned her face back to him. "But seriously, dollface, he hurt you?"

Summer felt all gooey as she stared into the concern. It had been a while since anyone had cared. "No, Teddy. He didn't hurt me. I swear. I think he just wanted to hook up, and he wasn't really getting my very loud and very clear message that I wasn't interested."

Instead of relaxing, Teddy seemed to tense even more. If he clenched his jaw any tighter he was going to need a dentist. Her hand absently drifted toward his jawline and stroked. Her body and her brain were clearly not communicating well. When she realized just what she was doing, she started to pull away. But Teddy grabbed her wrist and held it in place.

They stared into each other's eyes for what felt like hours but was probably only seconds, her fingers brushing up and down over the stubble on the side of his face. In turn, his thumb lazily stroked the pulse point on her wrist.

Wait. What the hell is happening?

"Um, Teddy," one of the bartenders called out as he poked his head out of the back exit, "I need some help in here; we're slammed."

Summer was back on her feet seconds later, heading back toward the bar. What had she been thinking? He must think she's a psycho. Chucking lamps at his head one minute, then stroking his face like a horny Frog Hog the next. She was definitely a hot mess. She needed to pull herself together. Quickly.

***

Summer let out a sigh as she slumped back into the deckchair. Picking her wine glass back off the table, she couldn't help but chuckle at the refill Laney had poured her. It was splashing over the sides before it had even made it to her mouth.

"Thank God you're not working with me at Mickey's, Lanes, this measure would have got you on Teddy's shit list for sure."

Her friend threw her a devilish smirk, her dark eyes twinkling. "What can I say? When it comes to wine, more is more."

God, Summer had missed her friend. It was a small miracle that they always managed to pick things up from where they'd left off. She was more than aware that traveling for work and being away for long periods of time didn't make her the best bet when it came to friendship. And she was sure most people would call her out for the lack of actual communication while she was away. It wasn't like she didn't keep in touch. She did. When she could. And trading memes totally counted.

"How is it, working with Teddy?"

That was a good question. Since her first shift where she'd practically pawed him like a cat in heat, she'd been avoiding him. Well, as much as someone can avoid someone they work with.

"Uh, yeah, it's okay. You know Teddy, ever the charmer … to everyone but me."

Laney grinned mischievously. "Oh yeah, I forgot that you were the Teddy whisperer."

Summer almost choked on her tongue. "Hardly! A whisperer means you can make them do things … like, oh, I don't know … be nice to you?"

"And him giving you a free place to stay and a job, isn't that him being nice to you?"

Well damn, when Laney put it like that.

After gulping some more of her wine, Summer decided Teddy was the last thing she wanted to think about right now. It had been hard enough trying to avoid him all week.

"Can we change the subject, please? Why don't you tell me how you managed to get Max and the kids out of the house long enough to drink with me?"

"Okay, I'll give you a pass … for now. We'll revisit the topic of Teddy when we're another bottle deep!"

Summer couldn't help but laugh, even though she knew her friend was far from joking.

"And as for the free house, well, let's just say Max was unable to resist my feminine wiles." Laney winked as she picked up her own glass.

Now that, Summer could believe. Laney was gorgeous. With her long, curly black hair, flawless dark skin, and a body that could easily make any model jealous, even after having two kids. Fortunately, her husband, Max, wasn't a stupid man. He knew what he had, and he would literally do anything for her. Including taking the kids over to their grandparents this evening and not returning until they were asleep. Effectively giving his wife a night off.

Summer and Laney drank, gossiped, and laughed until their sides hurt for the next couple of hours. Summer had tried to keep it light, but two bottles of wine later, her lips were loosening.

"So, why are you *really* back? And are you back for good? Don't think I haven't noticed you changing the topic every time I ask you about work."

She knew this was coming. It was only a matter of time. Ignoring the look her friend was pinning her with, she stared instead at the pristine lawn. They'd been sitting out on the deck ever since Summer had arrived, and sometime in the past hour or so the sun had gone down, leaving them with just the glow of the kitchen light to navigate the backyard. There was something so calming about sitting outside in the dark.

"Summer," Laney warned, "come on, spill."

Urgh.

"Okay, okay." Summer met her friend's eyes again. "I quit. You know what happened with Ben … well, even though we broke up a frigging year ago, the dude couldn't take the hint. He followed me on my last two assignments, and, well … well, I just had enough."

She was leaving a few things out. But that was still the most she'd told anyone so far.

"What?" Laney screeched. "You can't just quit your job because of that asshole! You love your job. You love working for the aid agency. Traveling around. Helping people. Making a difference. Did you report him? That's harassment right there! He can't get away with that."

Summer smiled at her friend's outrage on her behalf. But it really wasn't necessary.

"It's fine, Lanes. Really." She reached over to place a hand over Laney's. "Yes, I loved my job, but the plan was always to come back here. Back to Bluestone. Permanently. I'm not gonna lie, Ben following me around and generally being a douchebag definitely made my decision to leave easier. And quicker. But I was always gonna come back."

Her explanation seemed to calm her friend … a little. That was until she had time to think up questions.

"But what are you gonna do here? And aren't you gonna get bored? You've been traveling the world for ten years for God's sake, and now what, you're just gonna find a nine-to-five in small-town Montana? I know you, Summer, you'll be bored shitless in a month."

"Well … I was planning on taking over Mickey's, but Teddy royally screwed me over there. So, I need a new plan. But I'm not gonna stress about it now. Having a roof over my head and a job means that I can take my time and think about my next steps. And trust me when I tell you, I won't be getting bored. Don't get me wrong, I did love my job. But I'm not getting any younger, and living out of a backpack gets old. I want to plant some roots. Start the next chapter."

Her friend eyed her for a moment. Obviously considering what to say next.

"Okay, girl, time for tequila."

And just like that, Summer felt a million times better.

CHAPTER THREE

"Yeah?" Teddy answered impatiently, still trying to work out who on earth was calling him so late at night.

He was still at Mickey's. It had been a long and busy day, and all he wanted to do was crawl into bed. But he had a feeling that wasn't going to be happening anytime soon.

"Um, hey, Teddy?" a man's voice he didn't recognize replied.

"Who is this?"

"Oh, it's Max."

"Okay …" Teddy asked slowly. He didn't know Max all that well. Certainly not well enough for the man to be calling him at midnight. Was he going to hurry up and get to the point of his call or what?

"Right. So … I'm calling about Summer." At the mention of Summer, Teddy's whole body went on high alert. "Her and Laney thought it would be a good idea to get shitfaced. And, um, well, they're not in great shape, if the ice cream covering my kitchen floor is anything to go by."

Teddy couldn't help but smile as he pictured a drunk Summer. "So … you need reinforcements or something?"

He heard the man on the other end of the line chuckle. "No, not exactly. Well, maybe. A drunk wife and two kids seem to be my tipping point. And Summer isn't exactly okay to be left alone … so I was hoping you could come get her? Make sure she's okay tonight?"

"On my way."

Teddy had hung up before Max even had a chance to reply. There was no time to waste. Summer needed him. Just the thought of seeing her had his blood pumping quicker.

After locking up the bar, he practically ran back to his apartment building where his truck was parked. It was a good thing he knew exactly where Laney lived. Not that he'd been stalking Summer's friends or anything since he'd returned to Bluestone. Or eavesdropping on any of their conversations when they just so happened to be talking about Summer. No. Definitely not.

Twenty minutes later, he was trying his best not to laugh his ass off at a very drunk Summer. He'd found her sitting on Laney's kitchen floor, and she was currently singing some song about tequila at the top of her lungs.

"Tequila! It makes me happy …" Summer hiccupped, humming for a moment before singing again. "Tequila … it feels finneeee. Tequila when the doors are opened, and tequila when they're calling time—"

"Okay, dollface." Teddy crouched down. Once he'd wrapped his hands around her waist, he gently pulled her to her feet. "That's it, up you go."

He continued to hold on to her as she rose to a standing position. It was clear from her Bambi legs that she wasn't going to get very far on her own.

"Teddy," she whisper-giggled, "do you like tequila?"

"Not as much as you do." Before she had a chance to reply, she was up and over his shoulder in a fireman's lift. It was the easiest and the most efficient way he could think of to get her outside and into his truck.

"Hey! What the hell!" Summer weakly protested. She flailed around for a second before going completely still and quiet. So quiet Teddy started to get worried.

"Summer? You okay?"

"I-I can shee your butt from here," she slurred. "Y-y-you have a nice butttt, y'know? I didn't realize men's butttts could be so-sooooo … muscley. Yours is all hard. But kinda-uh round still. Huh."

Jesus Christ.

He looked up at Max, who was trying to stifle a snigger as he held open the front door for them. Rolling his eyes, Teddy headed out and ignored the very inebriated woman over his shoulder, who was now trying to grab his butt.

A chin lift to Max later, and Teddy was opening his truck door and securing Summer into the passenger seat. Once he'd buckled her in, he rounded the truck and started up the ignition.

Summer was no less chatty on the drive back to his apartment. She asked him at least ten more times if he too liked tequila. Sang her tequila song off-key two more times. And just as they were approaching his car lot, she went back to commenting on his appearance.

"I like the-the stubble thing you got going on. It makes you … makes youuu look kinda manly. Like, you've got sooooooo much testosterone, no razor is—*no*! No razor *can* stop that beard from growing. Does that make sense? Oh, and what's with all the flannel shirts? You were always more of a jeans-and-tee kinda dude. Not that I don't like the flannel. I do. It's hot. You look like some kinda … some kinda … lumberjack … but like, a sexy one."

That he did laugh at. A sexy lumberjack?

"You think I'm sexy, huh?" After putting his truck in park, he turned to her with a raised eyebrow.

Instead of answering, she continued to stare at him. She was turned toward him in her seat, one side of her head resting against the leather. Her long, blonde hair was down and in disarray around her shoulders. Several buttons of her blouse were undone and the material was skewed to the side, revealing one bare shoulder.

Despite being wrecked and looking slightly disheveled, she was still the most beautiful woman Teddy had ever seen.

He could see the flecks of green in her glassy eyes more clearly and the rosy pink of her lips was more prominent. It was obvious now that no matter what form this woman came at him, he was powerless to resist. Angry, happy, sad, or drunk. She was always perfect. And he was screwed.

"Come on, dollface, let's get you inside."

"Why do you call me dollface?"

His smile widened. He might as well tell her. It's not like she was going to remember much in the morning.

"I call you that 'cause …" He let out a deep breath. "You have these beautiful, big, almond-shaped eyes. They look like they belong on a doll. Hence … dollface."

She won't remember me saying this, right?

She licked her lips, not taking her eyes from him. Just that innocent swipe of her tongue made him want to groan. She was killing him.

"Beautiful?"

"Yeah, Summer. Beautiful." He took a moment to compose himself before he said something else stupid. "Come on, let's get you inside."

This time when he carried her, he cradled her in his arms. Which he immediately regretted when she threw her hands around his neck and buried her head into his shoulder. She fit perfectly. Why did it have to feel so right? Damnit.

"Thanks for looking after me, Teddy," she muttered into his shirt.

"Always."

Once they were safely indoors, he lay Summer on his bed. Damn, if she didn't look good in there, which was the last thing he should be thinking about right then.

After taking off her shoes, he covered her with his warmest blanket and went to get some water. She was going to have one doozy of a hangover tomorrow.

Getting her to take a few sips was harder than he imagined. He ended up with more on his shirt than down her throat. Some water was better than none though. Realizing she wasn't going to drink anymore, he settled the glass back on the bedside table. In case she got thirsty in the night.

"Time to sleep now." He lightly brushed his knuckles over her flushed cheeks.

Sighing in contentment, Summer snuggled deeper into the blanket. "I love it when you touch me. Makes me feel all tingly."

Me too, darlin', me too.

"Go to sleep, doll." He kissed her forehead, yet somehow found the strength to drag himself away.

"Night, Teddy."

"Night, Summer."

Grabbing a blanket for himself, he settled in for the night in the armchair he'd dragged beside the bed. He needed to watch over her in case she needed him. Or had to vomit. Or so he told himself.

***

Teddy stared at his reflection in the bathroom mirror, Summer's drunken words from last night still fresh in his mind.

After making the swift decision to shave less and buy more flannel, he bent over the sink and splashed some more water on his face, the cold sting awakening the rest of his brain cells. He needed to pull himself together. He'd slept an hour at most. Instead of dozing off last night, he'd watched Summer sleep. Like some kind of weirdo. What the hell was happening to him?

A noise from the bedroom had him hurrying up. She was awake. And he was itching to go check on her.

Looking as good as he was going to get, he exited the bathroom. He didn't have to go very far to get a glimpse of Summer, as it was attached to his bedroom. He wasn't prepared for the sight before him. Although he shouldn't be surprised. The woman certainly had a habit of keeping him on his toes.

A grin tugged on the corners of his mouth. "Is there a reason you're lying on the floor, dollface?"

Summer's head came up and twisted to face him, her hair was sticking up in all different directions. It was really fricking cute.

"I fell," she weakly replied.

That must have been the crash he heard from the bathroom. Thankfully, she didn't look hurt. Just inconvenienced. "Okay … and it was just so comfortable you thought you'd stay down there?"

Letting out a groan, she let her head drop back onto the rug. "I'm too weak to move, Teddy," she whined. "I'm never drinking again. Why the hell did Laney let me drink tequila? She knows it's my kryptonite."

He couldn't help but chuckle as he remembered Summer wailing out the lyrics to her tequila song last night.

Her face was still buried in the carpet when she spoke again. "It's not funny," she grumbled.

She was wrong. It was definitely funny. Making his way over to the side of the bed, he hovered over her for a moment, trying to decide how best to help her up. She didn't seem to mind his new proximity. And when he reached around her waist to gather her into his arms, she didn't protest either.

"Come on. Up you go. You want back in bed, or do you wanna come in the kitchen and I'll make you something to eat?"

He could practically see her mind working. Every single thought changing her expression. She was still in his arms, and he had no plans to let go just yet. Even hungover, she managed to take his breath away.

"Food. But I feel gross. Can I use your shower?"

The thought of Summer naked in his shower had his body reacting. He could feel himself tense up. Even his jaw seemed to clench.

Jesus. Get your mind out of the gutter!

"Uh, sure," he grunted. "You want something to wear

too? Sweats? A shirt?"

Her eyes lit up at that, and she nodded enthusiastically. That was until another groan escaped her lips. "Urgh. Right, need to remember, no sudden movements. Sudden movements are bad."

So freaking cute.

It was a shame he had to let her go in order to get her some clothes. Reluctantly, he dropped his hands from around her waist and left her standing next to the bed as he went over to his drawers. After rummaging for a minute, he pulled out some sweats, which were most definitely going to drown her, and an old T-shirt.

As he passed her the clothes, he could tell from the blossoming smile on her face that he was never going to get them back. Not that he cared. The idea of her in his clothes brought out something primitive in him.

Yeah, you really need to pull yourself together man.

He watched her stumble into the bathroom and close the door before he dragged himself away. Coffee. He needed coffee. Maybe that would help him pull his head out of his ass.

Long story short. It didn't.

Having Summer in his space was making him feel like a teenager again. A boy with a crush. Only he wasn't a boy anymore.

So much for thinking his feelings for her were in the past. It was clear the Summer-effect was still as powerful as ever. Over the course of just one week, the woman had already turned his world upside down. She was living in his apartment. Working at his bar. Passing out in his bed when she was drunk. And now, here he was, cooking her breakfast. She was so far under his skin, it wasn't even funny.

"Hey."

Teddy peered up to see Summer approach the counter. She looked almost shy. Uncertain. His clothes swamped her small frame, but he couldn't deny he liked seeing her in them. Her hair was still wet, leaving damp spots over her shoulders and down her chest. She looked good. Fresh. And best of all. She smelled like him.

Caveman much?

"Hey," he returned and gestured to the breakfast stool, "take a seat. I'm making your favorite—omelet with cheese, ham, and green peppers."

"You remembered?" She gasped.

"Of course." How could he forget? The morning he'd left for the Navy, she'd taken him to Dotty's diner for breakfast and went on and on about how any other type of omelet sucked.

A small smile pulled at her lips. Was she thinking about that morning too? Her face as she waved him goodbye would always be engraved into his memory. Leaving her that day was harder than leaving his nan and pops.

She kept her eyes on him as she slipped onto the chair. "About last night ..." she started but abruptly stopped as he asked, "How you feeling?" at the same time.

They both let out a short laugh. Returning to the frying pan, he gestured for Summer to carry on while he made her food.

"Yeah, uh, I'm okay. Nothing a little food and some Advil won't take care of. I was gonna say, thank you. For, y'know ... coming to get me and ... for looking after me. I'm not gonna lie, a lot of last night is still a bit of a blur, but I ... I remember you taking care of me. Sort of."

Teddy glanced up to see her fiddling with her fingers. It was the first time he'd ever seen her look so unsure of herself. Was it him? He found himself shaking his head at his own stupidity. Of course it wasn't him. She's hungover. That's all.

"Sort of?"

"Yeah." Another short and shaky laugh escaped her lips. "I ... well, it's kinda coming back to me slowly. Like horrifying, drunken flashbacks."

"Oh yeah? And which parts were horrifying?" He

couldn't keep the amusement out of his tone.

He could see heat start to flush her cheeks as she bit down on those luscious pink lips. She must be remembering some of what she'd said. Trying to be a gentleman, he averted his eyes and concentrated on serving up breakfast. Once he'd set a plate in front of her, he turned back to pour her a fresh mug of coffee.

"I'm pretty sure you're well aware of the horrifying parts, Teddy. I'm sorry though … for what it's worth."

Coffee served, he studied her for a moment while he sipped on his own drink. The breakfast bar she was seated at was his favorite part of the kitchen. It was a simple floating island with a marble top and four stools scattered around it. But what made it look really good right now was Summer sitting there.

Taking a seat next to her, he breathed in the scent of his soap on her. God, she smelled good.

"What are you sorry for?"

She glanced over at him, her cheeks pinkening all over again. "I said some stuff … and I'm fairly certain I grabbed your ass. I'm really sorry. Drunk Summer is obviously a little bit handsy."

Teddy's smile was so wide, it should have hurt. "No need to apologize, dollface. You're welcome to grab my ass whenever the mood takes you."

Obviously unprepared for that particular response, Summer started to choke on a piece of omelet. His hand automatically went to her back where he started to pat her as she continued to cough.

"Water. You want water?"

Shaking her head, she chose to take a sip of her coffee instead, which surprisingly seemed to do the trick. Even though she'd recovered, there was a lesson to be learned: his flirting needed some serious work. He was so out of practice, he was now a choking hazard.

After mumbling how fine she was into her mug, she went back to eating. This time in silence. In fact, the room was so quiet Teddy could hear his own heartbeat. And it didn't sound very healthy.

Five whole minutes went by before either of them spoke. The tension in the room was so thick that a knot formed in his stomach and tightened with every passing moment.

This is dumb. Say something. Anything.

"Uh," he quickly rushed out, "it's your day off today, right?"

Did my voice just echo?

"Uh, yeah." Summer pushed her now-empty plate aside but kept her head down.

"Up to anything special?"

Up to anything special? That's the best you can think of? Seriously?

"Um, y'know, just the usual, life admin stuff. Uh, yeah, actually it's getting late, I should get going. Let you get on with your day." She was on her feet and backing away from the counter before he even had time to digest her words. And by the time he was standing, she was already out of the room, shouting her goodbyes as he heard her gather her things.

A moment later the front door banged shut.

"Well. That was fucking awkward."

CHAPTER FOUR

Summer was mortified. No. Mortified didn't even begin to cover it. It was worse than that. It was "changing your name and leaving the country" bad.

When she'd first woken up at Teddy's, there were a lot of blanks. It hadn't taken her long to remember getting shitfaced with Laney. The dry mouth, pounding headache, and nausea were a bit of a giveaway. She wasn't even surprised she'd woken up at Teddy's. It made sense that either Laney or Max called him. And being the man he is, Teddy had stepped in to be her knight in shining armor. But the night before was blurry at best. Until it wasn't.

The more time that went on, the more she remembered. Which was why she was currently hiding under a blanket on her couch. As if she could physically hide from all the embarrassing things she'd said and done.

Yeah right.

A knock on her door had her peeking up from the woolen cover. She wasn't expecting anyone. It was her day off. Thank God. Besides, the entrance to her apartment could only be accessed through the back of the bar, so it wasn't exactly easy for people to show up unannounced.

Maybe it's one of the bar staff. Or Teddy. Oh God, please don't let it be Teddy.

Crawling off the couch, she winced as each step toward the door rattled her still-pounding head.

"Ivy! What are you—"

Ivy jumped into Summer's arms with enough force, it managed to back her further into the apartment. "Summer! It's been forever! I can't believe you're back!"

Once Teddy's sister finally untangled herself, Summer had a chance to get a good look at the woman she'd become. Her long, dark hair was tied into one of her signature braids. As usual, she looked effortlessly beautiful in just jeans and a vest. But there was something different about her. She was glowing.

"You're looking really frickin' fine, girl." Summer beamed and reached for her hand, pulling her further into the living room. "Come on in, I'll make us some coffee."

Ivy followed her into the connecting kitchen and leaned against one of the granite counters. "Coffee sounds great. How long are you back for? I would've been by sooner, but Teddy only told me you were back today! Can you believe that? When he mentioned you'd been back a week, I swear to God I almost punched him. *A week. A whole week,* my dumbass brother doesn't tell me you're back in town. You must have thought I was being so rude not coming to see you."

Summer couldn't help but smile. Ivy liked to babble when she was flustered, it was good to know that hadn't changed. She realised then just how much she'd missed Ivy. She was like the little sister she never had. Even though there was only a few years difference in their age, Summer had always felt protective of her, and that would never change either.

"Don't be silly, you're like the least rude person I know." She passed Ivy a mug and grabbed her own. "I'm sorry I haven't managed to come over to the ranch to see you yet. Teddy mentioned that it's doing really well and—" Summer's eyes widened. "Oh my God, is that what I think it is?"

Ivy's smile was dazzling as she lifted her left hand and allowed Summer a closer inspection of the ring. "Yeah, I guess it is. I kinda met someone."

"Holy shit. That's the biggest emerald I've ever seen! You marrying a prince or something?"

Her friend giggled. "No, not a prince. His name is Ace. He's friends with Brady Mitchell—you remember him, right? Well, they served together. You're gonna love him, I know it."

"Yeah, I remember Brady; how's he doing?" Talk about a blast from the past. "Oh, I'm sure I'll like him. If he makes you smile like that, then he's already got my vote."

"Oh, Brady's good. He's a cop now and married. You're gonna love his wife, Ali, she kinda reminds me a bit of you. Oh, and her sister, Lily. Lily's married to Jake McAllister— you remember him too, don't you? Well, you'll love her too." Ivy paused for a second and then excitedly screeched, "I know! We should arrange a girls' night so you can meet them. I'll set it up! You're working at Mickey's now, aren't you? It will have to be on one of your nights off. Hmmm. Okay. I'll plan it. You still haven't told me how long you're in town for? Please don't say you're leaving soon?"

Summer tugged on Ivy's hand again and led her back into the living room and onto the couch. Summer had a feeling seating would be required for the type of catch-up they were about to have. Once they were both settled into the cushions, Summer put Ivy out of her misery.

"I'm not leaving anytime soon. In fact, I'm here to stay. Permanently. And yes, I'm working here. And yes, a girls' night sounds good. I can't wait to meet them. *And* your man. Brady and Jake were always great guys, I'm glad they found equally great women."

Ivy opened and closed her mouth several times before she finally said something. "You're staying here? For real? You quit your job?"

Letting out a slow breath, Summer nodded. "I did. I'm

back. For good.”

Ivy launched herself at her once again and hugged her so tightly, Summer struggled to breathe for a moment. “That makes me so happy Summer, you have no idea. Does Teddy know you're staying? For good, I mean.”

“Yeah, he knows, why?”

“Oh, uh, no reason, just wondering.”

Ivy was never the best liar. But for now, Summer would let it slide. She was more interested in learning more about Ivy's ranch, her fiancé, and her new friends. So that's what she did.

***

Mickey's was bustling. It felt like the whole town was out tonight. Which meant they were slammed behind the bar. Summer couldn't even remember taking a breath in the last two hours, let alone a break.

After her last wine order though, she realized pretty quickly there was a problem. They were low on clean glasses. They'd obviously been pouring quicker than the glasses were getting cleaned and restocked. She knew she needed to leave Teddy and Kelly behind the bar and do a round. Mission Collect Empty Glasses was on.

Spinning around to face Teddy as he poured yet another beer, she didn't have to wait long to garnish his attention.

“What's up?” He side-glanced her.

“I need to do a glass run ... you gonna be okay back here while I'm gone?”

She knew he would, but it didn't mean she didn't have to ask. “Good thinking. Yeah, Kels and I will be okay. I forgot to mention that Jacob is on his way in too to help us out.” He took a minute to scrub his free hand over his stubble before fixing those big green eyes on her again. “I don't know what in the world is going on tonight, or where all these people are coming from, but thank you. I'd be screwed if you weren't here, or if you weren't so damn good."

He was killing her.

"You don't have to thank me, Teddy. I work here ... remember?" She smiled, knowing full well it didn't reach her eyes. "Be right back, boss." She threw in a wink for good measure. Maybe that would sever some of the intensity off that relentless gaze. Spoiler alert. It didn't.

Squeezing through the crowd, Summer grabbed as many empty glasses as she could. In one very ninja-like move, she even managed to curl her body around an occupied corner table to pick up the empties settled along the window ledge.

For her fourth and final trip, she decided to tackle the area around the pool tables. Located at the very back of the bar, the two tables were always crowded. Even if people weren't playing, it was a place where they liked to linger. She knew before she got there this would be where she would find the majority of glasses. Maybe even enough to keep them stocked up for the rest of the night.

Summer mentally high-fived herself when her eyes roamed over dozens of pint glasses scattered across the nearby tables. Jackpot. The happy high crashed and burned as soon as she caught sight of Colt though. He was already stalking toward her before she'd even gotten the chance to collect one glass. If the leery look in his eyes was anything to go by, this wasn't going to be good.

Oh dear.

With every step he took, she took one back. She stupidly thought if she dodged and weaved he'd give up. Get the message. He didn't. Within seconds, Colton's hands were on her hips, maneuvering her against the wall. As he used his six-foot-two frame to shield her from sight, a familiar feeling of helplessness trickled through her. She hated feeling vulnerable. Hated that he could easily overpower her. Hated that she was scared. She never used to be like this. The old Summer wouldn't have been shaking like a leaf. No. She would have no problem screaming in his face, calling him every name under the sun, and kneeing him in the balls. Where was that Summer when she needed her?

"What do you want, Colt?" Even her voice was wobbling. God, she was pathetic.

"Dang, Summer, you're looking hot tonight." She flinched as Colt dragged the tips of his fingers down her cheek. "God, I missed this face. It's been too long since I touched this silky-soft skin of yours." His eyes openly perused her body before returning to her face. "We were really good together. We had a lot of fun too. Remember that time at the lake?" When she didn't reply, he carried on. "I do. I remember peeling that sexy-as-fuck bikini off you and taking you right there on the bank."

She was going to be sick. "We've been over for years, Colt." That sounded better. Stronger. Firmer.

But her newfound strength didn't last all that long. His thumb went to her mouth and stroked her lower lip as he dipped his head, allowing his whiskey breath to sink into her skin. "All the more reason to get to know each other again. Refamiliarize ourselves with each other's bodies. Huh?"

"I'm not interested, Colt." Her breathing was coming out in pants now. "Please let me go. I-I need to get back to work." She struggled against him, but he didn't move a muscle.

Instead, he got closer, pressing his body so far into her until they were touching from hip to chest. Goddamnit. She knew she should scream. Hit. Push. But she couldn't. She was frozen in place. What was happening to her? What had Ben turned her into?

"I bet I could have some fun convincing you, babe." His dirty smirk made her shudder. "Don't think I've forgotten what that sexy little body of yours looks like while you're writhing around beneath me. Tell me you don't miss me. Huh? Tell me you don't miss me pounding into that tight—"

Thankfully, his words were cut off before she could throw up. His big body was wrenched from hers and tossed aside like he weighed nothing more than a rag doll. She felt relieved but still couldn't move. She could take in the scene before her though. Teddy. Of course, Teddy had saved her. Summer was getting damn good at being the damsel in distress.

"No means no, asshole." Teddy growled as he picked Colt up by the scruff of the neck. "You ever, *ever*, lay one fucking finger on her again … I'll carve you up into tiny fucking pieces and feed you to the fucking dogs. You understand me, asshole?"

Jesus.

She watched as Teddy practically threw Colt across the room. "Get your ass out of here and don't ever come back."

With the help of his friends, Colt was dragged out. But Summer was still shaking. Still frozen. She tried to focus on her breathing, which had somehow gotten wilder.

Teddy noticed. His hands were on her shoulders as he did his thing, assessing the situation. Assessing her. Soothing words in a gentle voice washed over her as he forced her to slow down her breaths.

"That's it, dollface. Just breathe with me, okay? In … and out. That's it. You're doing so well. Again. In … and out. That's it."

Moments later, she was in the air, cradled in his big, strong arms, and being carried toward the back door to her apartment. It had been a long time since she'd felt this safe. This protected. She was still trembling, but at least her breaths were evening out. Though that also meant that it was only a matter of time before mortification set in.

CHAPTER FIVE

Summer hadn't stopped shaking and Teddy was reluctant to let go of her. As soon as he'd closed the door to her apartment, he'd taken her over to the couch and sat down while she remained cradled in his arms. She was currently perched in his lap, her face buried in his shoulders. Still goddamn shaking. He was trying his best to soothe her. But right now, he felt helpless. All he could do was hold her and hope it was enough.

That asshole ex of hers was going to pay. Teddy had been too lenient on him downstairs. His fist should have been in Colt's face the moment he dared to touch Summer. That and the filth he was spurting to her was unforgivable. What gave him the right to speak to her like that? Prick.

The most concerning thing though was that he'd never seen Summer react like this before. Not to anything. He liked to think he knew her pretty well. They'd grown up together. Spent an ungodly amount of time with each other. Seen each other at their best and at their worst. But this? This he'd never seen. Something was up. Something had changed.

It was a while before Summer spoke. When she did, her trembling was just beginning to subside. Nonetheless,

Teddy kept a tight hold of her. His touch seemed to have calmed her, so he wasn't about to let her go.

"I'm sorry," she croaked into the crook of his neck.

"You've got nothing to be sorry for." His hand unconsciously began stroking her back. "How you feeling?"

She lifted her head, and he got his first look at her since he'd carried her inside. She looked almost … scared. "I-I'm okay." She quickly ducked her head again and went to crawl off his lap, but he didn't let go.

"Dollface, look at me." When she kept her head low, he tried again. "Please. Look at me, Summer."

Slowly turning her attention back to his face, he watched her throat muscles work as she gulped. "I'm okay, Teddy. Thank you for … y'know. I'm really sorry. I know it's busy and the last thing you needed tonight was to—"

His finger went to her soft lips to halt the nonsense she was sprouting. "Summer. Like I said before, you have nothing to be sorry for. You didn't ask for that asshole to harass you. This is on him. Not you. Understand?"

She nodded but looked no less upset. In fact, her beautiful eyes began to swell as they filled with water. Tears cascaded over her flushed cheeks, and Teddy felt his heart constrict. He was helpless again. Pulling her back into him, he let her sob into his shirt, continuing to stroke her and offer her words of comfort. He hoped like hell he wasn't making things worse. Crying women had always been his weakness. But a crying Summer could bring him to his knees.

Teddy didn't know how long they sat there. It could have been minutes or hours. But he vowed to stay there for as long as she needed him. When the tears eventually dried, he decided to try and talk to her again.

"Tell me what's going on in that pretty little head of yours, dollface."

When she didn't immediately reply, his heart began to sink. But then she surprised him. "I was scared. I know it's stupid, but I thought … I thought …"

His stomach twisted. He didn't have a good feeling about where this was going. "What did you think, doll?"

She was quiet for so long Teddy thought she wasn't going to answer. When she finally spoke, her words made his fists clench. "I thought he was going to hurt me."

His mind went back to that bruise on her arm. "Who hurt you, Summer?" He tried to keep his voice calm, but the anger inside him was bubbling to near boiling point.

Every single muscle on her body tensed. That's when he knew. Some asshole with a death wish had dared to lay a hand on her. His Summer.

"I-I … Can we not do this tonight … please? I'm tired. So tired."

Luckily for Summer, Teddy was a patient man. He might not get all the details tonight, but he would make sure he did eventually. Sooner rather than later.

Tightening his grip on her, he pulled himself up and off the comfortable couch cushions and strode toward the bedroom. It was time for her to rest. As he lay her down on the white sheets, she gripped his shirt, preventing him from pulling back.

"Will you stay?" Her voice was nothing but a whisper.

"Sure, doll, if that's what you want. I can sleep on the couch."

"No." She wiggled up onto her elbows. "In here. Can you stay in here with me? Please." He watched her take a deep breath before she met his eyes again. "You make me feel safe."

Whoever the person who hurt her was, he was a dead man.

He swallowed down the lump in his throat and reached for the wrist that was still clinging to his cotton shirt. "If that's what you want Summer, that's what you'll get. Now, let's get these shoes off, yeah?"

Slowly dropping her hand, her head slumped onto the pillow. She already appeared visibly calmer from the knowledge that he wasn't going anywhere. Teddy tried hard not to read too much into that. She was just shaken, and he was familiar. That was all.

Focusing on the task at hand, he removed Summer's shoes and then, at her request, her jeans. Soon, she was in nothing but a tank top and bright red panties.

Now is not the time to drool. She's scared. She literally just had a panic attack in your arms. She needs you to take care of her, not check her out.

The idea of Summer scared was enough to curtail his libido. Thank God. Once his own boots were off, he left his clothes on and joined her under the quilt. She came willingly into his arms and rested her head on his chest. Everything about it felt right. This was where she belonged.

"You'll always be safe with me, Summer," he whispered into her hair.

Feeling her snuggle deeper into him, he felt himself smile into the darkness.

***

"You know she's staying, right?" Ivy was not being subtle. She hadn't shut up about Summer since he'd arrived at Dotty's diner.

Pushing his now-empty plate aside, he leaned back into the squeaky red booth and eyed his sister. "And?"

"And … stop pretending you don't give a shit."

He crossed his arms over his chest and lifted a brow at her. "And what exactly makes you think *I do* give a shit?"

Ivy huffed and braced her hands on the steel-top table. Clearly already exasperated with him. She hadn't seen anything yet.

"Don't act dumb, Teddy. It really doesn't suit you. You've been in love with Summer Willis since fifth grade."

Love? Who was Ivy kidding? "You been reading those romance books again, sis?"

He felt her glare on him as he smiled up at a tired-looking Dotty who had chosen that exact moment to come over and clear their plates. The older woman took her time, and Teddy was thankful. It was the quiet before the storm if he was reading his sister's face correctly.

He was right. Once Dotty was out of earshot, Ivy laid it all out for him. "She's just as gone for you too, y'know? But you're both just so darn stubborn. So stubborn you're gonna miss the chance to actually be happy. Do you know how dumb that is, Teddy? Are you really gonna let your pig-headedness stop you from being with the woman you've spent your whole life loving? Huh? Are you? And don't even pretend she's not the reason you came back to Bluestone. Or bought her granddaddy's bar."

Teddy had stopped listening right after she'd said that Summer was gone for him too. Was that true? Or even possible? He thought back to two nights ago. The feeling of rightness that filled him as Summer lay curled up next to him all night. He'd snuck out in the morning, not wanting to embarrass her, but now he was beginning to think he should have stayed. Made sure she was okay. Seeing as she'd been avoiding him ever since, it was probably safe to assume he had done the wrong thing. Damnit. He was such a dumbass.

"Fuck." He scrubbed his hand roughly through his hair.

"What?"

"I think I fucked up."

"Um. Yeah! So … you gonna tell her how you feel? Finally?" Ivy took another sip of her coffee, still not taking her eyes off him.

"I'm not talking about that. I'm talking about the other night. At Mickey's. I spent the night with her but … I left in the morning without waking her."

Ivy spat out the gulp of coffee she'd just taken. Brown spray was now covering half the table.

"Jesus, sis. Drink much?"

"Teddy!" she screeched, bringing more attention to their table than he was comfortable with. "You can't just say shit like that and expect me not to react. Jesus. What the hell is wrong with you?!" Her voice dropped as she leaned over the table. "I can't believe you slept with Summer and sneaked out the next morning. That's fucking low. How could you do that to her? I ought to kick your ass on her behalf. Not to mention for all of womankind too."

Oh. He realized his mistake. Quickly. "Shit. No. Not like that. We didn't hook up, Ivy. She was upset. That asshole ex of hers Colt decided to corner her at the bar. After I kicked the douchebag out, I took Summer upstairs and looked after her. She was feeling a little ... uh ... fragile ... and asked me to stay. So, I did. To sleep. Nothing more. But the next day, well, the last thing I wanted to do was embarrass her ... so I left."

He was happy to see that his sister no longer looked homicidal as she relaxed back into her seat. But she wasn't exactly thrilled either. Nor was he. Saying out loud what had happened drilled home just how much he'd messed up.

"You need to talk to her. Like yesterday. And apologize for leaving. Blame it on being a dumbass man, I don't care, just say something. Hopefully ... she'll forgive you. You should know that right now, I reckon she's feeling way more embarrassed about you sneaking out than she is about breaking down."

Fuck a duck.

He needed to fix this.

***

It was Summer's day off and she wasn't at her apartment. Teddy knew because he'd checked. He'd also checked Laney's, and she wasn't there either. He'd not had any luck finding her in the shops or cafés around town. Which meant only one thing. She'd gone to their spot.

It had been years since he'd gone back there. Only venturing out one time when he first arrived back in Bluestone. Being there without Summer just hadn't felt the same. They'd discovered it together when they were kids, and it had been their retreat when life got tough. Hours had been spent there, talking, laughing, they'd even snuck beers out there.

Taking his truck, he braved the dirt roads past Moonrock Ranch, where he and Ivy had grown up, and toward the old Monroe plantation.

He parked up and started the ten-minute hike across the fields. For once, he was thankful for the drier weather. A few weeks ago, this would have been a much muddier trek. Spring had most definitely arrived, a fact he was more than aware of as his skin began to heat under his jacket.

It took a moment for Summer to notice him. When she did, he didn't miss the frightened jolt or the slight shake of her delicate fingers.

"I didn't mean to scare you." Teddy sank into the crisp grass beside her.

"What are you doing here, Teddy?" She sighed, not taking her eyes from the view in front of them.

You could see for miles up there. The mid-afternoon sun beating down on the palettes of green. If he looked closely, he could even make out Moonrock.

Taking in a deep breath, he let the fresh air fill his lungs. "I came to find you."

"Why?"

"I fucked up." He chanced a glance in her direction; she was still looking ahead of her. "I thought I was doing the right thing by leaving your apartment the other morning, but … I was wrong. I'm sorry, Summer."

"You don't have to apologize, Teddy. And I really don't need you feeling sorry for me. I know I freaked out the other night … but if it's all the same to you, I'd really rather just forget it, okay?"

Yeah right.

Like he could forget how she trembled and sobbed in his arms. Not to mention, his body had already memorized the feel of her warm skin plastered against him as she clung to him all night long.

He stayed quiet for a bit. She was obviously on the defensive, and he had no intention of riling her up. He just wanted to fix this. Make it right. And get some answers.

They sat quietly for a while, taking in the view. Once he was certain she'd relaxed a little, he decided to answer her previous question. "Why don't we start by you telling me who hurt you … and then I'll decide whether to forget it?"

Teddy felt her glare burning into the side of his face. Nope. Still prickly. "Sure, Teddy. I'll get right on that. But before I do, are you gonna tell me why you left the Navy? You know, the only job you've ever wanted? The one you gave up everything for?"

It was his turn to tense. Not even his sister knew the details of why he left. It wasn't a pretty story. Life wasn't always sunshine and roses. Not that he needed to tell Summer that. But still, he wasn't exactly in the mood for a heart-to-heart.

"Don't try and change the subject, Summer," he bit out, sounding harsher than he wanted.

"You want me to cry on your shoulder, Teddy? Hear all my secrets? Well, tough shit. It doesn't work like that. You want me to open up to you … then I damn well expect you to do the same."

She'd turned her whole body toward him now and sat crossed-legged in the grass. He decided to shift too and face her. There was no way he was ready to lay everything bare for her, but he could share just enough to get her to open up. He already knew there would be no other way. Ivy was right; Summer was insanely stubborn. Just like him.

"Okay. Fine. I left because on my last mission I was captured. I was a POW. Fifteen days in total. The longest fifteen days of my life."

"Shit. Teddy. I'm so sorry." Going to her knees, she did something he wasn't expecting, something very un-Summer-like. She threw herself into his arms and held on to him for dear life.

Immediately wrapping his arms around her, he let his

head fall into the crook of her neck. He breathed in the familiar notes of vanilla and ignored the tightening of his chest as he did. They stayed like that for a while. It gave him time to get his thoughts in order. He hated talking about what happened. Not that he'd spoken to very many people about it. His commander, his team, and a Navy-issued shrink were the extent. But even that had been hard.

He cleared his throat when she eventually pulled back. He tried his best to push down all the messy emotions threatening to spill over. He needed to stick to the facts. "Four of us were captured. Only two of us made it out alive. After that …"

I had a breakdown. I still can't sleep without seeing my teammates' blood-stained faces. I thought about giving up in more ways than one.

The words sat in his throat. There was no way he could say any of them out loud. As if sensing his struggle, Summer took pity on him.

"It wasn't the same," she finished his sentence for him. "I get it now. I'm so sorry that happened to you, Teddy. Truly, I am. And if you ever need to … you know … talk. I'm here. Always."

He was surprised and relieved that she wasn't pushing him for more. "Thank you." As raw as he felt, he hadn't forgotten his reason for sharing. "Do I get to hear your story now?"

He patiently waited while Summer shifted uncomfortably on her butt. She was purposely avoiding his gaze, choosing to focus instead on picking at the material on the end of her sleeve. She was quiet so long, he was worried he needed to prompt her again, until she whispered a name.

"Ben." Teddy already hated him. "We worked together. At first I thought he was a nice guy. I mean, he worked for an aid agency for God's sake. You'd think that in itself would weed out the assholes."

"But he wasn't," Teddy unnecessarily added, already knowing the answer.

"No. He wasn't. And by the time I realized how *not* nice of a guy he was, we were already dating. Had been for a while."

Swallowing down his anger, Teddy reached out and curled his hands around hers, which were now trembling.

"One night ... we'd just gotten back to our room after a really long day, and he was mad. Really mad. I'd never seen him like that before. He started accusing me of flirting with one of the other workers, saying I'd embarrassed him. I didn't know what on earth he was talking about ... and you know me ... never one to shy away from a fight. Well ... I never used to be."

Now her whole body was shaking, and he couldn't take it. He hurled her into him again, this time, positioning her onto his lap. The need to hold her was undoubtedly stronger for him than it was for her, but he didn't care. He knew what was coming, and he needed to be holding her when he heard it.

Once she'd snuggled her head into his shoulders, she carried on. "I called him a jealous asshole, among other things. Let's just say he didn't take it well. He pulled me by the hair and slammed me against the wall. Then slammed me again. Over and over. I was so shocked. I couldn't believe what was happening. I can't even remember saying that much after that ... other than telling him that he was hurting me."

Bile rose up from Teddy's stomach. She'd been in a relationship with this man. She'd given him her trust and he'd abused it. The son of a bitch had laid his hands on her. While she'd been alone, in the middle of nowhere. Goddamnit. How long had she been stranded with this abusive asshole?

The other night at Mickey's made sense now. That motherfucker had scarred her. Messed with her head and made her feel less than. Teddy wanted nothing more than to hunt him down and give him a taste of his own medicine. But before he did that, he needed to hear the rest.

"What else? What happened after that, doll?"

He hadn't felt or heard her cry, but the tears seeping into his shirt alerted him to the fact she was. "I-I ... I was an idiot. Once he'd calmed down, I tried to leave, but he ... he begged me to stay. Literally, on his knees, begging. At one point he started crying, saying all the right things, like how he didn't mean to hurt me, he'd never do it again, begging me to give him another chance. All that crap."

"So you stayed." It wasn't a question, but she answered it anyway.

"Yeah. I stayed. And he did it again. And again. The fourth time, I left. Managed to transfer out. I was fine for a while, but then ... he found me. Followed me to my next assignment. And the assignment after that." Teddy's grip on her tightened. "He'd send me messages too, crazy messages. Threats, insults, pleas to take him back. You name it, he said it. You have no idea how many times I've had to change my fricking phone number." He heard her voice crack. "When he managed to get another few bruises in, I decided enough was enough and I quit the agency altogether. Came back here."

"You quit because of that asshole?" Teddy's blood was boiling.

"No. Well, yes and no. I was ready to leave; I guess he was just the last straw. The kick I needed to get out. No pun intended." She managed to force out a short laugh, but there was nothing funny about the situation.

"His last name?"

"Huh?"

"His last name, dollface, what is it?"

Drawing back, her hazel eyes flashed in defiance. "Oh no. Don't you dare, Teddy McCallen. I did not tell you all that so you could go all Rambo on me. The last thing I need is you getting locked up because of that asshole."

Holding up his hands defensively, he couldn't help but smile at the light that had returned to her eyes. "Rambo is not my style, doll, and I promise you that I'm not about to get myself locked up. I just want to know his name, that's all."

A cute little snort escaped as she shook her head at him. "That's all, my ass. No frigging way."

Looks like he wouldn't be getting any more information from Summer. Oh well. No matter. It wouldn't stop him from finding the bastard.

CHAPTER SIX

Summer could not believe she had spilled all the sordid details of her relationship with Ben to Teddy. Even Laney, her best friend, was in the dark about what had happened. Summer was ashamed. Embarrassed. How would Teddy be able to look at her again without seeing the pathetic, weak woman Ben had turned her into?

She could feel the sympathy coming off him in waves. He'd been glued to her side ever since he'd found out. Most women wouldn't complain about having a beautiful man follow her around like a puppy dog. But she wasn't most women. And Teddy McCallen certainly wasn't most men. He was *the* man. The only man she'd ever wanted more than anything else in the world. So seeing the look of pity on his handsome face wasn't exactly doing wonders for her self-esteem.

I am not a charity case.

No matter how many times she told herself that, one look at Teddy hovering around her, told her differently.

"Get out of here, Kels. Summer and I will finish up," Teddy called over to Kelly, who was stacking the chairs onto tables.

The young woman smiled over to them both. Obviously

worried Teddy would change his mind, she hightailed it to the back room to gather her things in record time. Less than a minute later, she was out the door.

Alone again.

"There a reason Kelly's getting special treatment, Teddy? You've never offered to cut short my shift before," Summer joked as she continued to wipe down the bar.

He didn't answer. Instead, a large bottle of whiskey was plonked down in front of her. Confused, she looked up to see Teddy on the customer side of the bar, grinning.

"Time for a break, dollface. Grab some glasses and get your ass over here."

Never one to turn down a free drink, Summer made quick work of gathering the glasses and rounding the bar. Teddy had already poured a generous amount of the muddy liquid by the time she'd settled onto the stool next to him.

"What are we drinking to?" She held up her glass in preparation to toast.

"To friendship."

She beamed back at him and clinked his glass with hers. "To friendship."

Yep, friends. Other friends want to rip the other's clothes off and trace every hard ridge of their chest with their tongue too, right?

As the night went on, Summer undertook pouring duties while Teddy made small talk. And that's all it was. Small talk. The topics were so mundane, they might as well have been talking about the weather. But that wasn't the problem. Not really. The real issue was the not-so-innocent brown liquid warming her insides. Because it turns out, downing whiskey shots with this man, whatever she should call him—boss, friend, man she'd been in love with since she was twelve— was not a good idea. Hell, three drinks in and she was practically ready to strip naked and beg for him to touch her.

Desperate much?

"Doll? What do you think?"

Shit. What's he talking about?

Teddy's deep chuckle echoed around the empty bar.

54

"Am I boring you, dollface?"

"No! I'm just … uh, sorry … I missed what you said. I'm listening now, I promise. What do I think about what?"

"I was asking if you were up for going over to Moonrock tomorrow? Ivy and Ace are having some sort of shindig." When she didn't immediately reply, he shrugged and continued. "I thought it might be cool. You've not been over to the ranch in forever, and Ivy's really done a lot with the place."

"Are you going to be there?" There was no way she was going without him to a shindig full of people she didn't know or hadn't seen in God knows how long.

He smiled at her question. A smile so distracting it should be illegal. "I'll be there. So … you up for it?"

"Sure." She took another gulp of her drink, savoring the smoky tang. "You might have to remind me though, I'm a few drinks in and there's a good chance I'll forget this conversation entirely." She was only sort of joking. She'd become a lightweight.

Teddy's eyes lit up. "Is that so? So, I could say anything to you right now and you'd forget it in the morning?" He sniggered before draining the contents of his own glass.

"Let's see, shall we … Truth or drink? No harm if I'm gonna forget, right?"

"Hell yeah. That means I've got blackmail material for future use."

She laughed right along with him while he lined up shot glasses and filled them to the brim. Maybe she was a little drunk. Teddy blackmailing her wasn't very funny.

Shit. Was this a bad idea?

It was too late though. She'd have to chastise herself later. All she could do now was concentrate on not humiliating herself.

"Okay." Teddy rubbed his hands together. He was way too excited. "We'll start off with the easy stuff. I'll go first." Why wasn't she surprised? "Best memory?"

A small smile tugged at her lips. "That's an easy one.

Senior year. Bobby Rhodes was spreading rumors about hooking up with me and I was about ready to lose my mind. You wanted to cheer me up, so you convinced me to play hooky and we spent all day driving around. We also ate a shit ton of junk and ended up in our spot, blasting Green Day and drinking some weird minty liqueur that you'd stolen from your pops."

That was a good day.

Teddy stared at her so long she began to shift in her seat. His scrutiny was unnerving. She'd expected him to laugh, reminisce maybe, or at the very least crack a smile. He was doing none of those things. Instead, his eyes bore into her with such potency, she didn't know where to look. Finally, she couldn't take it anymore.

"What?"

He stayed quiet for what seemed like an eternity. Eventually, he managed to snap himself out of it. Shaking his head, he ignored her question and simply said, "Your turn."

Did I miss something?

"Uh, okay. Fine. Biggest lie you've ever told?"

She watched his mind work as he contemplated her question. He did that thing he always did when he was unsure: he ran his hand over the top of his head, ruffling his short brown hair enough to make him look like he'd just woken up.

"Remember the day I left for the Navy, we had breakfast that morning?" He waited for her to nod. "You asked me if there was anything you could've done or said that would've changed my mind about joining up. I said no, but that was a lie."

Summer's breathing hitched. She remembered that day as if it were yesterday. The image of Teddy driving away, forever etched in her mind. She remembered asking him that question too. It was intended as a joke, even though a part of her was still hoping he'd change his mind.

Her heart pounded as she waited for him to continue.

Suddenly she had to know the answer.

"Teddy …" She trailed off, realizing she had no clue what to say next.

"The truth?" He paused for a moment. "You. The answer was *you*."

"What?" Her voice was just a whisper. He wasn't making sense.

"If *you* asked me to stay, Summer … then I would've stayed. For you."

Did he just say what I think he just said?

There was no playfulness in his tone. It was scarily serious. And back came that stare. She searched his features for a smile, a smirk, a lip twitch. Anything. But there was nothing there.

"Why?" The question was out of her mouth before she even had time to contemplate whether she really wanted to know the answer.

"You know why, dollface."

"I do?" *Has he lost his mind?*

"You're really gonna pretend that you didn't know I had a crush on you?"

"What?" *He had a crush on me?!* "What are you … I don't understand … how was I supposed to … y-you never said anything? I mean, you dated other girls."

Teddy let out a laugh. But there was no humor in it. "Dated? Who the hell did I date? Huh? Come on … tell me? In all the years you knew me growing up, name one girl I supposedly 'dated'?"

"Becky Matthews." Summer didn't even hesitate to throw the name out there. The day she'd heard Teddy had slept with Becky, she'd locked herself in her room and cried all day and night.

"Becky Matthews?" he repeated, giving her an incredulous look. "I did not fucking *date* Becky Matthews."

"Okay. Fine. You didn't date her, but you *did* sleep with her."

"What the hell are you talking about, Summer? I didn't

fucking sleep with her. I didn't fucking sleep with anyone in high school! I went into the Navy a goddamn virgin. Did you not hear me when I said I was gone for you? Why the fuck would I sleep with some chick when I was into you?"

She couldn't breathe. Her head was throbbing. He hadn't slept with Becky. Or anyone. He'd actually had feelings for her, the same feelings she had for him. None of this made sense.

"She told me you slept together. *Were* sleeping together." Her voice remained quiet while the pounding of her heart felt anything but.

"She lied, Summer."

What the ever-loving fuck?

"I have no idea why. Probably the same reason Bobby Rhodes lied about you two hooking up."

Their eyes locked as she processed his words. She wouldn't have been able to look away from him even if she wanted to. "Why didn't you tell me?"

"About Becky?"

She watched Teddy's head tilt.

"No." Her head shook profusely, losing his eyes for a moment. "About how you felt. All those years and you never said anything. Why didn't you say anything?"

At her words, he stood. His barstool scraping against the vinyl floor. Suddenly, he was in her space. One of his meaty thighs slipped between her and opened her jean-clad legs to him. The next thing she knew, his hand was at the back of her neck, gently tilting her head up while holding her firmly in place at the same time. The other hand was cupping her face, a callused thumb lazily stroking her cheek. What was happening?

"I tried once." His face edged closer until his breath was tickling her lips. "After my first deployment. I came back here. To you. But when I got here …"

"Colt," she whispered.

Stupid Colt. No one was ever going to measure up to Teddy. But after learning about Becky, she figured he just didn't see her like that. After, of course, he went and joined the Navy and left her in Bluestone. Alone. And then, at her lowest, in swoops Colton. It wasn't her proudest moment.

His green eyes flared at Colt's name. She watched in fascination as anger quickly dissolved and was replaced by lust. Seconds later, his pupils dilated and darkness overtook. His gaze darted to her mouth where she'd had the sudden urge to run her tongue along her lower lip.

Before her brain fully understood what was happening, his mouth was crashing down onto hers. There was no way she was going to waste any more time thinking now. Not when the taste of Teddy was sending her into sensory overload. His teeth scraped and tugged on her lower lip until she gasped. Once her mouth was parted, his tongue swept inside. Slowly, he explored, gliding back and forth, easily taking control of the kiss.

The more he teased, the more goosebumps broke out across her skin and the foggier her mind became. To keep herself steady, her hands went to his sides, inadvertently pulling him closer to her. When his thigh moved and pressed into her core, she couldn't help but whimper.

His hands didn't move, they simply kept her in place, occasionally tilting her head so he could take her deeper. Her hand movements though were less controlled. They slid to the front of his shirt, her fingernails digging into the hard ridges of his chest, as if she was checking to see if he was real. Going by the guttural groan vibrating from his stomach, Teddy seemed to approve.

His thigh pressed into her again. This time it was harder. She had the sudden urge to rub herself against him.

No. Bad Summer. Control yourself, woman.

She swallowed another growl-like noise Teddy made and knew right then she was in deep shit. Teenage Summer may have been smitten, but thirty-four-year-old Summer was screwed. This man had the power to break her, as in crumble into a million tiny pieces that no amount of superglue could fix.

The minute her brain switched back on, in time for her to contemplate just how screwed she was, Teddy's exploration had slowed. As soon as his lips left hers, she drew in a deep breath. Now very aware of just how oxygen-deprived she was. That's why she was breathing so hard, right?

With one last gentle caress of her cheek, he not only pulled away, but he also took a step back. Damn if that didn't hurt. The instant loss of his heat made her shiver. At least that's what she was telling herself.

"We have to stop." His voice was gravelly. Harder. Rougher than she was used to.

Of course. They'd been drinking. This wasn't a good idea. Oh God, was she taking advantage of him? Suddenly mortified, she scrambled up and off her stool. She didn't miss how wobbly her legs were when she stood. It would take a while before she recovered from that kiss. There was also a possibility that she wouldn't. Not ever.

"Uh, yeah, I should—" Summer started but was soon cut off.

"No, dollface. Don't run." His arms wrapped around her as he pulled her back into his big body. She found herself looking up again, staring back into those mesmerizing eyes. "Don't think for one second I *want* to stop, Summer. I don't. But if I feel you moan into my mouth one more time while I'm feasting on those cherry lips … I'm not gonna be able to control myself."

Oh. Well, shit.

"Yeah, oh," Teddy grunted out. Wait, had she just said that out loud? Apparently whiskey was hell on her filter.

She didn't know what to say. Talking in her head clearly wasn't safe either. She needed to get out of there. Pull herself together. In private.

Carefully unraveling herself from his hold, Summer attempted to take a step back, but Teddy was right there. He didn't touch her, simply moved with her, his gaze holding her in place.

"I mean it, Summer. Don't run from me. You think I've waited this long to taste you, only to let you leave?"

She involuntarily gulped at the hunger she saw in his eyes.

"It's late. Go to bed. I'll come by at one tomorrow to pick you up and take you over to the ranch. We'll talk. I'll kiss you. We'll enjoy our day. And then I'll kiss you again."

Well, all righty then.

The smile he graced her with made her wonder if she had just said that out loud too. Yes. It was definitely time for her to go to bed.

CHAPTER SEVEN

That kiss. That goddamn kiss. It was something else. Better than he'd imagined. And he'd imagined plenty. It had also gone from PG-13 to X-rated pretty damn quickly when Summer had pushed herself into the thigh he'd not so innocently placed between her legs.

Kissing her hadn't been a part of the plan last night. He'd been finding it hard to leave her side ever since he'd found out about her scumbag ex, and he was hoping to talk to her more about how she was really doing. How that descended into truth or drink, he still didn't know. But he couldn't deny how happy he was. After that kiss, everything was now crystal clear. Summer was his.

She hadn't come right out and told him how she felt, but that kiss said it all. The way she melted into him. Dragged her nails down his chest. Mewed into his mouth. It was all Teddy needed to take the next step. Operation Make Summer His. They'd wasted too much time already. Well, no more.

After knocking on Summer's apartment door, he held his breath. He had no idea what to expect after last night. Was she going to retreat? Pretend nothing happened? Or was she going to throat-punch him for taking advantage of the situation? You never knew with Summer. It was part of her charm.

When the door did fly open, all rational thought went out the window. Her dirty blonde hair was down, and she was wearing some sort of clingy dress thing. The dark green an exact match for the flecks in her beautiful eyes. She'd paired the dress with flat black ankle boots. Jesus. She looked hot.

Screw going slow.

"Hi." A corner of her mouth tipped up into a smile as she noticed his perusal of her. She knew exactly what she was doing to him.

He didn't reply. Instead, he closed the distance between them and dipped his head. Hearing her breathing hitch made him feel ten feet tall. It also allowed for those pretty pink lips to part. And he was going to take full advantage. Again.

As soon as his lips touched hers, he felt the same jolt of electricity that had pulsed through his veins last night. She tasted of mint and coffee and something uniquely Summer. Something sweet and tangy enough to make his skin tingle.

She made that sexy sound again as her tongue tangled with his, and he swore he could feel his blood heat. His body was more than happy to spend the entire day there. Like this. Taking exactly what it wanted. Needed.

Unlike last night, his control faltered, and his hands began to wander, dragging down the sides of her sexy-as-hell dress. He memorized every curve his fingers dipped in and out of. They settled on her hips. His grip was firm as he pulled her flush against him. Enjoying the feel of the moan she made as he swallowed it down.

When Summer's hands began to roam over him, he let out his own groan. She wasn't gentle with her exploration. She grabbed his biceps and squeezed. Once she was satisfied, her fingers then went to his chest, where she ran her nails down his torso. It was like she was marking him as hers. And he damn well loved every second of it.

It was Summer who pulled away this time. He reluctantly released her lips and sucked in some much-needed air. They were both breathing hard. Teddy would go as far as to call it panting. He still managed a smile though. Especially when he got a look at her dazed expression and swollen red lips.

"Hi," he belatedly greeted.

"Jesus Christ, Teddy, give a girl some warning before you kiss her like that," Summer replied, still breathless.

Somehow, he felt his smile get wider. "What can I say? You bring out the beast in me."

A blush crept over her cheeks. Now, this was a side he'd never seen before. Summer Willis shy? No freaking way. This was going to be fun.

"Come on, doll." He took her hand and led her out the door. "It's time to get this show on the road."

***

It would seem, Ivy's little get-together was a couples' thing. A fact he would've liked to have known before bringing Summer over. It wasn't that he didn't want to be a couple with her. Or hold her hand and pull her into his side, like the other men seemed to be doing with their women. He did. But he recognized that it was too soon. They'd shared a total of two kisses and had zero discussions. The last thing Teddy wanted to do was spook her. She was skittish enough already.

The usual gang was there when they'd arrived. Ivy and her fiancé, Ace. Ace's best friend, Brady, and his wife, Alice. Alice's sister, Lily, and her husband, Jake. And finally, Jake's sister, Sam, and her husband, Duke. Couples. Everywhere.

They'd been at Moonrock for a few hours already. As soon as they'd arrived, Teddy, with the help of Ivy, gave Summer a tour of the ranch. Ivy and Ace were horse breeders and in the past year they had managed to triple their clients with the help of Ace's brother. The success meant they'd finally been able to update the stables and give the main house a makeover. It was safe to say, it no longer looked like the house his grandparents had brought them both up in.

Lily and Alice had dragged Summer away over an hour ago, claiming they needed some girl time. Teddy didn't mind. Mostly because she was still in his eye line, and the sight of Summer smiling and laughing was something he'd never get tired of looking at.

"You know, she's not going to magically disappear if you take your eyes off of her?" Ivy came to his side and leaned against the same wall he was resting against.

"You sure about that?" Even as he spoke, his eyes remained fixed on Summer.

He heard his sister snort. "I take it something has happened between you two?"

"And why would you think that, sis?"

"Well, firstly, you can't keep your eyes off her. Not that that's anything new. But at least before today, you were pretty subtle about it. Now, you're just blatantly staring at the poor woman. Not giving a damn if she or anyone else knows you're doing it." Ivy had a point. "Then there's the tiny detail of you basically admitting to me that you were in love with her the other day." He did no such thing. "Then all of a sudden you turn up with her. Here. And you're looking at her like that."

He turned to face Ivy, her hands were still flailing, and she was even more animated than usual.

"Something might've happened. But …" He needed to tamper down the excitement he saw flare in his sister's eyes. "It's literally just happened. As in last night. We haven't even had a chance to talk about it yet."

"Okay …" Ivy replied slowly, "I take it you made your move and kissed her or something?"

God, she was nosy.

That was enough sharing for today. Time to change the subject. "How about we stop talking about my love life and you tell me when exactly that fiancé of yours is gonna make an honest woman out of you?"

He grinned as Ivy slapped him on the arm and growled. "Bloody caveman. You're more obsessed about us setting a date than I am! It's the twenty-first century, bro, I'm not about to be exiled if I'm not married and with child within the year."

"What's this I hear about you being married and with child?" Ace boomed from behind her. He wasted no time wrapping his arms around Ivy's waist and dragging her back into his chest.

Teddy was used to their public displays of affection. All the couples there were the same. Sickeningly happy. He just wished he had the right to pull Summer into his arms whenever he felt like it.

One day. I just need to be patient.

"Teddy was asking, *again*, if we've set a date for the wedding," Ivy informed Ace as she leaned her head back and rested it against him.

Ace chuckled, the mottled skin on one side of his face creasing as his smile widened. As a former marine, Ace had been a victim of a nasty car bomb, which had not only ended his career in the military but had also left him with burns covering the left side of his upper body and face. Teddy hardly noticed the burns anymore on his soon-to-be brother-in-law. It wasn't like Teddy didn't have his own scars. His time as a POW left him with more than he could count. But unlike Ace, they were all safely hidden under his clothes.

"Hey, don't look at me, man." Ace laughed. "If it was up to me, we would've made it official the day I proposed. Your sister is the one taking her sweet ass time setting a date."

"Getting cold feet, sis?" Teddy grinned.

"Hey!" Ace protested.

"No!" Ivy quickly reassured her fiancé. "It's just the idea of planning a wedding makes me want to go and lie down in a dark room."

"Then let's go down to the courthouse? Or we could

elope … fly to Vegas like Jake and Lily did?"

"Who's eloping?" Summer's sweet voice called out as she strolled toward Teddy.

Without thinking, he instinctively pulled her into his side. It wasn't until after his hand was flexing on her hip that he realized what he'd just done. In front of Ivy and Ace. Fortunately, Summer either hadn't noticed or didn't mind. He was hoping for the latter.

"Ace wants to be married like yesterday, while the thought of planning a wedding makes Ivy want to hurl," Teddy explained.

"I can help!" Summer excitedly did a little hop. "I'm not exactly a wedding planner, but I managed a load of events while I was working at the agency. I'm thinking a romantic backyard ceremony right here at Moonrock. Surrounded by close family and friends. What do you think? Nailed it, right?"

Her enthusiasm was clearly contagious because seconds later Ivy was jumping up and down with her.

"Oh my God, that sounds perfect," his sister beamed. "You'd really do that? Help me, I mean? I have no idea where to start and not a lot of time if this one over here has his way."

Teddy tuned out the conversation after that and enjoyed the sight of an excited Summer as she began listing off ideas. He knew Summer, as an only child, had always seen Ivy as the little sister she never had. They'd always got along as kids, but there was something special about seeing them get close as adults too.

***

Four hours later, Teddy was hovering outside Summer's front door. The afternoon had consisted of them both stuffing themselves silly with an obscene number of burgers and hotdogs while Summer and the rest of the women talked wedding plans.

After she'd allowed him to hold her to his side, Teddy had taken it one step further and taken hold of her hand as they left. Even once they'd arrived back at Mickey's, she hadn't protested when he'd laced his fingers through hers as they walked through the bar and upstairs. Even though they had reached her door, Teddy still hadn't let go.

As they stood quietly outside her apartment, it was obvious that they were both just as nervous. Teddy watched in fascination as a flush started to creep up Summer's neck. He would never get tired of seeing this shy side of her.

"Uh, do you wanna come inside?"

Yes. "No." One look at the hurt flashing across her face had Teddy rushing to explain. "I mean, I do. Of course I do. But that control I was talking about not having last night hasn't magically appeared. And that sexy as fuck dress you're wearing is not helping. If I go inside, I'm gonna kiss you. And if I kiss you, I'm gonna wanna touch you. And if I touch you, I'm gonna—"

"Okay," Summer cut him off with a smile, "I get it."

"I really hope you do, doll, 'cause I don't want you to think for one second that I'm not desperate to go through that door with you." Satisfied she understood what he was saying, he continued. "I know we didn't get a chance to talk about what's going on between us … but I'm gonna lay it out for you. I like you. I liked you when we were kids and I like you now that we're not. And going by the sounds you made while my tongue was inside of you, I think you like me too." That flush had now progressed into a full-blown blush. "I wanna see where this thing between us can go. So … tomorrow night, I wanna take you out. On a date. What do you say?"

"Okay."

"Okay?"

"Yes, Teddy, okay. I'll go out with you."

That was easier than he thought. "Thank God." He let out a heavy breath. "Seven good for you?"

"Seven is good for me. Where are we going? So I know

what to wear."

"Dress casual. Jeans or something."

Once she nodded her agreement, he dropped his head and lightly brushed his lips against hers. It was a chaste, closed-mouth kiss. He hadn't been joking when he said he wouldn't be able to control himself. After a whole day with her, seeing her laugh, touching her waist, holding her hand, he was hanging on by a thread. He needed to go home and sort himself out before he embarrassed himself.

"Sweet dreams, dollface."

CHAPTER EIGHT

This seemed like such a good idea at the time.

Summer and Ivy stared down at the piles of wedding magazines open in front of them. They'd hijacked a table at Mickey's for their planning session and were currently trying to decide the basics. Flowers, cake, and food.

When Ivy suggested coming over to make a start on planning, Summer had happily agreed. She needed the distraction. And to stop thinking about Teddy. Unfortunately, she hadn't thought the whole planning in the bar thing through. Even though it was her day off, Teddy was working the day shift and she hadn't missed the frequent glances in her direction. It was distracting. *He* was distracting.

And, damnit, the man could kiss. There could be an alien invasion happening around them, but if Teddy's mouth was on hers, she knew without a doubt she wouldn't know or care. The real doozy though was the revelation that he'd been just as gone for her as she'd been for him. Neither of them had said anything though or made a move. The whole Becky and Colt thing didn't exactly help, but they weren't to blame either. This whole screwed-up mess was on them.

"So … you gonna tell me what's happening between you

and my brother?" Ivy piped, interrupting her Teddy-filled thoughts.

"What?"

"You *know* what, Summer. You've both been making googly eyes at each other for the past hour. Now spill."

For God's sake.

Summer took a sip of her Coke before shooting Ivy a glare. "We have more important things to talk about, Ivy. Like, say, a sit-down meal versus a buffet-style spread. Have you decided what you'd like yet?"

She watched as her friend sassily flicked her braid over her shoulder. "Fine. Buffet-style spread. Now, stop changing the subject and tell me what's going on with you and Teddy?"

Summer let out a sigh before relenting. She knew Ivy well, and the woman was not going to let this go. "If you must know, we have a date tonight."

Ivy let out a little squeak. "I knew it! I frigging knew something was going on. Oh my god, I'm so excited. You're already like a sister to me ... but if you and Teddy got married, then you really would be my sister!"

"Jesus Christ, Ivy, Teddy and I are *not* getting married! It's *one* date. Our *first* date. Can you not marry us off just yet, please? The last thing I want is for you to get your hopes up and it doesn't work out between us."

Or I get my hopes up and it ends up falling apart like all my other relationships.

"Oh, I already know things are gonna work out. You and Teddy are meant to be. You always have been."

Summer could feel her face contorting. It was more than likely displaying a *what the hell are you talking about* expression.

"Don't look at me like that. You two have been circling around each other for years, and don't even try to deny it. You've both liked each other for a long time, but you've both been either too stupid or too stubborn to do anything about it."

There was really nothing to say to that. Summer wisely

decided not to argue. "Now that you've got that off your chest, can we talk about the flowers?"

Ivy groaned and dramatically flopped her head down onto the scratched wooden table. "They all look the same," she whined. "I like blue, just choose some blue ones for me."

Summer could do that. Blue it was.

***

Summer really shouldn't have been surprised that a date with Teddy would be unlike any other she'd had. Yet, she was. She still had no idea where they were going, but it was safe to say, it definitely wasn't to dinner and a movie.

They'd already driven further into the woods than could be considered socially acceptable for a first date. If she had been with anyone else, she would be calling the cops right about now. She wasn't an idiot. This was exactly how those serial killer shows started.

The long drive was also giving her time to think. And that wasn't a good thing. Her messed-up mind was high-fiving her one minute for bagging a date with Teddy McCallen, and then listing all the reasons that this wasn't a good idea the next.

Summer snuck another look over at Teddy; he looked hot, even more so than usual. He'd exchanged his usual flannel shirt for a black button-down and rolled his sleeves up to reveal the black ink on his forearms. She still hadn't gotten a good look at all his tattoos or even asked how far up they went. Of course, the best way to check would be an up-close-and-personal inspection. That sounded like a good time. Teddy McCallen shirtless. Okay, now she was squirming in her seat.

"Do I wanna know what's put that look on your face, doll?"

Busted.

It was official. The burning she felt on her cheeks meant

only one thing: her face was flaming. Even being caught red-handed didn't deter her dirty mind. At this point, it was safer to stay quiet. She didn't have a smartass retort. Or an innocent explanation. There was only filth lingering on the tip of her tongue.

What in God's name is wrong with me? Actually, don't answer that.

She really needed to get her mind out of the gutter and give herself a good talking to. This wasn't okay.

Teddy's deep chuckle had her head snapping back toward him. "Fuck, you're cute."

Cute? Since when did she become cute? She supposed Teddy wasn't used to seeing her blush. Or at a loss for words. But that's who she was now. She'd changed a lot in the years since they'd known each other. The past year had been especially brutal. Her confidence had definitely taken a nosedive, that was for sure.

Needing to steer the conversation into safer territory, she cleared her throat and managed not to say anything dirty. "You gonna tell me where we're going yet? Also, will there be food there?"

Another rumbly laugh echoed around the truck's cab. "You hungry, dollface?"

"Uh, yeah. I need to eat three meals a day, Teddy. It's basic biology. They don't teach you that at SEAL school?"

"Nah, I think I missed that one at BUD/S. I didn't miss the other biology classes though. The more advanced ones. I'd be happy to give you a demonstration of what I learned later?"

She smiled at that. "Are you gonna ask if you can unzip my *genes* next?"

A bark of laughter ripped through him. "No. But I might ask if you wanna decrease your dopamine and increase your prolactin together." He glanced her way and gave her a cheeky wink. She couldn't help but laugh right along with him.

She liked seeing him like this. He was so relaxed. Chilled.

Like he offered up biology-based sexual innuendos on the daily. There was also the advantage of his gaze remaining fixed on the road ahead, giving her a chance to shamelessly ogle him without being caught.

"You're such a nerd."

"Yup." His grin was infectious. Everything about him was.

Yeah, I'm screwed.

A few more nerdy puns later, they were pulling off onto a dirt road. Other than someone's house up ahead, they were surrounded by nothing but fields. As they got closer, realization set in. This had Teddy's name written all over it.

"Oh my God." She turned to look at him as he parked up. "You did it. You're building it."

Engine off, he twisted to face her, excitement glittering in those green eyes. "You remember?"

How could she forget? A cabin in the middle of nowhere. The ultimate dream for any dedicated introvert. Summer and Teddy had spent hours together detailing their perfect hideaway. It would have to be in the middle of nowhere. A cross between a cozy log cabin and a traditional farmhouse. She'd imagined dark wood floors and thick rugs. A real wood-burning fireplace. And, obviously, a view to die for.

She stared at the timber logs through the windscreen. He was really doing it. "Of course I remember. You're getting your bolthole in the boonies. How long?"

The outer shell looked near completion, with the exception of the wrap-around porch, which was still a work in progress.

"A couple of years. I'm getting there. Hoping in another six months or so it'll be ready." He opened the driver's side and jumped down. "Come on, I'll give you a tour."

He was next to her door moments later, helping her out. "You're doing it yourself?"

"What I can, yeah, but plumbing and stuff like that, I'll need to call someone in."

A house built by Teddy. I wonder if he'll let me watch him work? Topless.

Before they went inside, he snagged a torch from the back of the truck. He shrugged at her raised eyebrow and grunted out, "No electric yet."

They walked up what Summer assumed would soon be steps and through the thick wooden door. Evening light was fading fast, so despite the big bay windows in the front room, it was hard to make out details without the torchlight.

"Is that a real fireplace?"

"Yup."

Okay, now she was jealous. "Please tell me you're not planning on laying down dark wood floors?" He was quiet. Too quiet. "Oh my God, you are, aren't you?"

No answer. He just dished out that deep, rumbly laugh and started heading toward the arch at the far end of the room.

"Teddy McCallen, do not walk away from me!" She stomped after him, ready to tell him just what a thieving jackass he was, but her words died in her throat.

"This is gonna be the kitchen." Teddy's light was directed at the floor-to-ceiling windows that took up the whole back wall.

Summer could feel her jaw go slack. The view. That was something they both wanted. And what a view he had. Even as the sun set, she could make out the hills rolling in the distance like a picture-perfect postcard. Then there was the narrow creek that she could almost hear beating against the rocks.

While she'd been gawking, she'd walked closer to the windows. Her hand had even shot out, as if she could touch the pretty in front of her. Heavy footsteps followed and came to a halt beside her.

"Beautiful, huh? It's why I bought the place."

"It's perfect, Teddy. Just like you talked about."

"Just like *we* talked about," he corrected.

When she turned to face him, he was staring at her. A

look she couldn't decipher scrunching his features. "Show me the rest?"

A nod later, Teddy took hold of her hand and led her through the rest of the house. In every room, she could see just where everything would go. It was much bigger inside than it looked on the outside. He'd crafted four decent-sized bedrooms upstairs and one even had a ginormous ensuite. As jealous as she was, she was happy he had this. He deserved this. And he sure as hell had put his heart and hard work into it.

Once they were back in the front room, her stomach decided it was time to protest. A rumble reverberated around the very quiet room, and before Teddy had a chance to laugh, she shot him a glare.

"Come on, time to feed you."

As he led her back outside and toward the vehicle, she was momentarily confused when he didn't climb in. Until she spotted the blanket in the bed of the truck. Dropping her hand, he got to work laying down the chequer wool for them to sit on. After gesturing her up, he reached for something behind her and reappeared with a basket in hand.

"A picnic," she excitedly clapped. "Hell yeah, what did you bring?"

Once he'd climbed in and settled next to her, he started unpacking, Summer's eyes growing wider with every item he produced. It was all her favorites: bakery fresh bread, cheeses, cold cuts, strawberries, peanut butter cups, and, finally, sweet tea. The good kind, filled with sugar.

"This all right?" She could hear the concern in his voice. She hadn't said anything. She was too busy trying not to drool.

"You got all my favorite things." She managed to drag her eyes away from their feast and back up to the gaze of an entirely different kind of feast. "I can't believe you remembered. You even got me the fancy prosciutto."

He whipped out that sexy chuckle again. "Only the best for you, dollface."

As they began stuffing themselves, they fell into easy conversation. They talked about the house, Summer's grandfather, and Ivy and Ace's wedding. Safe topics. What they didn't talk about though was them. What they were doing. The fact that this was a date. The dilated pupils that made what little green left in Teddy's eyes murky as hell. And they definitely didn't mention the sparks flying around all over the place every time they accidentally grazed each other.

Now that she was full of food, it was harder to tell what was twisting her belly. The six peanut butter cups she'd just stuffed into her mouth, or the silence that had now fallen between her and Teddy? It didn't feel easy anymore.

Say something! Anything. Come on. You're making it weird.

She was drawing a blank. Food packaging was stuffed back into the basket, and then Teddy got closer. Soap and musky cologne filled her throat. There was no way she'd be able to think of something to say now, not when her brain had all of a sudden become fuzzy. She must have looked like a deer in headlights as Teddy leaned his big body toward her. A big hand went to cup her face and tilted it toward him.

"Have I told you how good you look tonight?"

Still at a loss for words, she weakly shook her head in response.

His hand slowly moved until his fingers were in her hair. "Well, you do. Every single fucking day, you take my breath away. You always have, Summer."

His forehead pressed into hers. "Teddy …" It was barely a whisper, which stopped as soon as she realized she had nothing to say to that. Thank you didn't exactly feel appropriate.

"It's always been you."

She felt the words hit her heart hard. Damnit. He was killing her. She may not know what to say, but she could show him how she felt. She captured his lips. Slowly. Gently. She explored. All the while Teddy held her firmly in place, the grip in her hair tightening.

Her tongue trailed along the seam of his lips, practically begging for him to open for her. Satisfaction pooled in her stomach as he did. She tasted, sucked, and nibbled before she allowed their tongues to tangle. As soon as they touched, Teddy took control. She gave it willingly. A quiver making her whole body shake as a feral sound ripped through him.

Her fingers went to his chest, where she clung hard to his shirt. She must've been pulling him closer to her because moments later both of his hands had slipped down to her waist. With one tug, she was hauled onto his lap and rearranged until she was straddling him.

Clearly Teddy didn't think they were close enough, as seconds later his grip on her tightened until she was pressed into him. No air in sight. She didn't have time to register just how hard he was all over because there he was, scrambling her brain again as he deepened their kiss.

Her body was on fire. This man. She never wanted to stop. She needed more. She needed all of him. It was playing havoc with her self-control. But right now, with Teddy's lips on her, with his big hands holding her in place, she couldn't bring herself to care. Who cares that she was moaning into his mouth? And who cares if the rocking on his lap was borderline inappropriate? She didn't. Wouldn't. It felt too good.

"Jesus Christ." Teddy's deep voice only made her blood heat more. "You're so fucking hot." He drew back slowly and let his lips run across her jaw and up to her ear. "I've fantasized about how you'd taste, you know."

She managed a whimper in reply. Her whole body shivered under his tongue as he trailed it along the shell of her ear. "How you'd feel. Against me. Under me. Over me." His teeth nipped her earlobe before resuming their journey and scraping down the side of her throat.

"Fuck," she panted. Because words were still failing.

"How you'd tremble. Just like you're doing now." He

sucked on that sweet spot at the nape of her neck. She was a goner.

Arching back, she let out a sigh. Teddy McCallen was going to be the death of her. But what a way to go.

His mouth wandered while her hands explored the ridges under his shirt. They were both panting now. At least she wasn't the only one losing her mind. But it would seem his willpower was much stronger than hers. Just when she was ready to throw caution to the wind, he stopped. She almost sobbed when he pulled back.

"Doll …" It felt like a warning. "We can't … not like this."

She knew deep down he was right, but her body was not on board. She might've still been rocking.

"Baby, fuck, you're killing me."

He leaned into her and took her lips again, but it was nothing like it was before. This kiss was excruciatingly soft and light. It was an ending rather than a beginning.

This time when he stopped, she did too. He was right. Not like this. Not in his truck on their first date. She'd waited too long, and he was too damn special.

CHAPTER NINE

Four times. Four times he'd been called out today. Apparently a whistling Teddy was a creepy Teddy. He wasn't going to argue. Not when he was this damn happy.

He was still reeling from taking Summer Willis, his dream girl, on a date. Summer had actually moaned into his mouth. Put her hands on his body. Rocked on his lap. Nothing. Not one goddamn thing was going to take away his good mood today.

"Jake," Teddy greeted as the man removed his Stetson and carefully placed it on the bar counter.

"Teddy." Jake nodded, running his hand once over his shaggy brown hair.

"What can I get ya?"

"Just a soda, I'm driving. Just waiting for Lily to close up the store."

Sounded about right. The stern, serious rancher was a marshmallow when it came to his wife, Lily. Every morning Teddy watched Jake drop off and pick Lily up from the hardware store across the street that she owned. It was as if the man couldn't stand being away from her a second longer than he had to.

And you don't feel that way about Summer?

Leaving that question for later, Teddy went about fixing Jake's drink.

"So, you and Summer, huh?"

Teddy couldn't help but chuckle. It had been one day. Guess you can't keep a secret in this town. "Wow. News travels fast. Let me guess, Dotty?"

"Actually, Lily. She heard it from Alice, who heard it from Ivy, who heard it from Summer. Our women tend to talk." A slow grin spread across Jake's sun-stained face.

The fact that Summer was the reason people knew, made his chest tighten. He'd been ready to shout it from the rooftops the first time they'd kissed, but he'd been waiting on her. For her to feel comfortable with people knowing. Apparently he needn't have worried.

"Good to know. In that case, yes. Me and Summer. It's still early days, but I'm happy, man." Teddy slid the soda over.

"I can see. Was that whistling I heard when I came in?" Jake let rip a throaty chuckle.

"Yeah, like you weren't sickeningly happy when you and Lily started hooking up?"

"I ain't about to deny it. So you're hooking up then?"

Jesus. How did I manage to put my foot in my mouth straight away?

Teddy rubbed his neck. "Uh, nah, not hooking up. We're uh … taking it slow. Well, actually, I don't know how we're taking it. But it's been like one date."

Could he have sounded any more panicked? Jake seemed to take pity on him. "I get it, man, don't worry. Word of advice though, from one old man to another?" Teddy grunted a "sure" before Jake continued. "Lily and I took it slow … if you know what I mean. And I gotta say, I'm happy as fuck that we did. See, it gave us a chance to get to know each other. Like really get to know each other. And by the time we took that next step … well, it kinda solidified what we'd built, if that makes sense?"

"I already know Summer pretty well; we grew up

together." He didn't know why he was confirming this. It wasn't like the man didn't know. Everyone knew.

He watched patiently as Jake slowly took a sip of soda and swallowed it down. "I get that. But you know her as a friend. Not someone you're dating. Not a girlfriend. Or a woman you're in love with. Trust me, you're both gonna need time to adjust. She ain't your friend anymore, Teddy. Unless you stick your tongue down all your friends' throats … in which case, I'm gonna have to seriously rethink that barbecue invitation." He was back to grinning now.

"Smartass." Teddy's hand had moved from rubbing his neck to messing up his hair as he pushed through the short strands. "Okay, I get it. You're right. I want to move us forward out of the friend zone, but not so fast as to freak her out."

As he was thinking about all the ways he was going to gently move their relationship forward, Jake downed the rest of his drink. It wasn't until the glass clinked back on the bar that Teddy looked up again.

"Happy for you, man. Glad to see you finally pulled your head outta your ass and made your move. Took you long enough."

***

Later that night Teddy wasted no time making his next move.

Teddy: *I'm taking you out on Sunday. Will pick you up at 1.*

Summer: *Didn't we talk about this? You're supposed to actually ask me. I could be busy.*

Teddy: *It's your day off??*

Summer: *Right. But what if I decided not to spend the day staring at my phone, waiting for you to call?*

Teddy: *Did you?*

Summer: *Teddy!*

Teddy: *Summer!*

Summer: *You're annoying.*

Teddy: *Summer. Can I please take you out on Sunday? I miss you. When I'm not with you, I spend the day staring at my phone waiting for you to call.*

Summer: *Fine!*

Teddy: *So you didn't have plans?*

Summer: *Don't push your luck, buddy.*

Teddy: *Night, dollface. See you at work.*

Summer: *Night, Teddy.*

Teddy settled back and rested against the headboard of his bed, his phone still in hand. It was late. All he wanted to do right now was sleep. But there was one more thing he needed to do. His monthly call to Tyler.

It had been going on three years, Teddy should be used to it. But the need to psyche himself up beforehand was strong. Even if it did make him feel guilty. Tyler was his friend. His brother. His teammate. And the only other person who could begin to understand the hell he went through in Iraq. Because he was there too. Four of them were captured, two survived. He and Tyler.

Ignoring the heaviness in his stomach, Teddy swiped down to Tyler's name and hit call.

"Is it that time of the month already?" Tyler sighed down the line.

"You missed me that much, huh?"

He heard Tyler mutter, "Like a hole in the head," before clearing his throat. *Charming.* "Let's get this over with, shall we? I'm fine, Teddy. Same as I was last month, and the month before that and the month before that."

"I ain't allowed to check in?" Teddy pushed down his frustration. They had the same conversation every month. Unfortunately for Tyler, Teddy was a stubborn bastard. He wasn't about to give up on his friend just because he found his calls annoying.

"Oh come on, Teddy. We both know you're not calling me to shoot the shit."

"I got plenty of shit to shoot, Ty."

"Oh yeah?"

"Yeah." *Fuck it.* "Remember the girl I told you about? Summer. Well, she's back in town."

The line went quiet for a minute, giving him just enough time to regret his attempt at a normal conversation. Their monthly calls normally consisted of surface-level pleasantries and nothing more. With Teddy usually gathering just enough information to reassure himself that his friend really was okay and wasn't about to do something stupid. They hadn't had any kind of heart-to-heart since they'd been back stateside.

"She is? Shit. You okay?"

Teddy puffed out a relieved breath. "Yeah, man, I'm good. You'll be pleased to know that I manned up and told her how I felt. Even got her to agree to a date."

"Was this like a gunpoint type of situation?"

"Fuck off." Teddy let his grin widen as his friend continued to rib him.

"Come on, man. Be real. You don't expect me to believe you won her over with that charming personality of yours, do you?"

"I'm a fucking delight, Ty, and you damn well know it!"

"Delusional more like." Tyler sniggered, sounding more and more like the carefree teammate Teddy remembered. It was good to know Ty was still there, lurking beneath the surface.

After a couple more jibes about his sunny disposition, Teddy decided to go all in. He told Ty about the date. What he was feeling. And even confessed how scared he was of royally fucking things up.

As Teddy listened to his friend's advice, he realized for the first time that he was the reason their relationship had deteriorated. All these years he'd been treating Tyler with kid gloves. Trying to stick to light topics. For fear of triggering him. He'd known the man a eight years but today was the first time in three years that he'd shared something personal with him. What kind of friend did that make him?

"I'm sorry, man," Teddy cut Tyler off mid-sentence.

"I'm really fucking sorry."

"What are you talking about?"

"I've been a shit friend, Ty. I might've checked in with you, but it's not escaped my notice that this is the first real conversation we've had in years. I'm a dumbass."

"Well, I'm not disputing that." Tyler paused, letting out a slow breath that muffled the line. "It's okay. I've not exactly gone easy on you. I know I can be an asshole."

"You? Never!"

"Ha-fucking-ha. Seriously though, man ... we're good."

Teddy felt something shift inside him. Could it really have been that easy to get his friend back? No. This was just the beginning. The first of many more normal conversations.

"So, when do I get to meet this Summer of yours? I gotta meet the woman that's had you twisted up in knots for more than a decade."

More like two decades.

"You think I'm gonna let your slimy ass near her?" Teddy chuckled. "I'll wait until I lock her down if it's all the same."

As much as he gave his friend shit, he was more than aware of Tyler's special skills with the ladies. It wasn't just the blond hair and blue eyes either, it was those blasted dimples. Teddy had spent years watching women fall victim to them. Over and over again.

"Scared of a little friendly competition?"

"Scared you're gonna scare her off more like ... with that ugly mug of yours."

Laughter erupted down the phone. That was more like it. This was what his friend had needed from him the whole time. Well, Teddy had plenty more jibes and a whole hell of a lot more real life to throw Tyler's way. Their monthly calls were about to get more interesting. Teddy even began thinking about his next visit.

Maybe I could take Summer?

As they continued to talk, hope bloomed in Teddy's

chest. The future was looking brighter by the second.

***

After a whole week of stolen looks across the bar and some pretty shameless flirting, Sunday had finally arrived. It was time for date number two. Teddy knocked on Summer's apartment door, no less nervous than he'd been all morning.

"Hi, dollface."

"Hey," she returned, a tinge of pink highlighting her cheekbones. "Uh, am I dressed okay? I didn't know where we were going."

Excellent. A chance to check her out without looking like a perv. Her hair was down and styled into loose curls, and other than a pink shade of lipstick, she wasn't wearing much makeup. As his eyes roamed over her flowy vest and tight blue jeans, he also noticed the signature black bracelets gathered at her wrists. He couldn't help but smile. She'd always had a hippy rock chick style going on. Eventually his gaze made it down to her scuffed black boots. She looked stunning. As usual.

"This is fine." His voice came out rusty, his body finding yet another way to betray him.

"Fine? That's all I get. Jeez, Teddy, give a girl a complex, why don't you." She failed to cover her smile as she grabbed her keys and locked up.

More than happy to take the bait, he immediately spun her around and pinned her to the door. Letting his hands drop either side of her head, he made sure she was locked in. He delighted in the sharp inhale she took and the fire he saw dancing in her eyes.

Not giving her a chance to speak, he dropped his lips on hers and gave her a proper hello. A demonstration so to speak of just how good he thought she looked and what exactly that outfit was doing to him.

They were both breathless by the time he drew back. It

wasn't an easy task, letting go of those luscious pink lips, and it was even harder not to go back for more once he got a look at how swollen they were from his kiss.

"You're looking really good, doll ... in case you were wondering."

Her eyes remained hooded as she struggled to reply. "Uh ... um ... thanks."

He reluctantly pulled back. Not touching her wasn't an option anymore though, so he settled on taking hold of her hand instead. A compromise. He then carefully maneuvered them down the stairs and through Mickey's, being sure to ignore the looks as they strolled out hand in hand.

"You gonna tell me where we're going?"

"Well ... first I'm gonna feed you. I recently found out that we're supposed to have three meals a day." Summer snorted, and he had a feeling she was also rolling her eyes. "Then we're going over to Moonrock. I thought I'd take you for a ride." He glanced over at her to see one eyebrow raised and quickly realized his mistake. "Uh, horse ride. We're going on a horse ride," he clumsily clarified.

Shit. Smooth, Teddy.

Why were his ears hot? Damnit. The woman made him feel constantly off-kilter.

It wasn't until they'd settled into a booth at Get Pied that he finally managed to pull himself together. He already knew what he was going to order, so it made sense to forgo menu browsing and instead drink in the sight of Summer's face lighting up as she studied the pie list.

"This place is awesome. Until today, I never knew I needed to be able to choose from fifty different types of pie. But now I know ... there's no turning back. I have no other choice than to try all fifty flavors."

Teddy felt his lips twitch. "No other choice, huh?"

"Nope. How am I gonna know which one I like best if I've not tried all of them?"

"I see your point." He stopped fighting his smile. "So, which one you gonna try today?"

Summer hummed for a little while, her eyes going back to the menu. "I'm trying to decide between lemon meringue, cherry, or pecan."

Teddy didn't get a chance to reply as their waitress arrived to ask if they were ready to order. It didn't matter though, he'd already decided. If his woman wanted three different flavors, then that's what she would get.

"We'll take a slice of the lemon meringue, cherry, pecan, and apple pie, please. And I'll get a coffee—cream, no sugar." He glanced over at Summer. "Doll, what do you wanna drink?"

"Oh, uh, a Coke for me, please."

As soon as the waitress was out of sight, Summer kicked him under the table. "Oh my God. Why did you do that? She's gonna think we're having some sort of pie-eating contest."

"'Cause you couldn't decide. Now you don't have to." He flashed her a toothy smile. "Besides, you need to make a start on those fifty, right?"

"I won't be able to eat three slices of pie, Teddy. Well, I could … but I won't be able to eat them all *and* go riding afterwards."

After letting out a chuckle, he reached across the table and took hold of her hand. "Don't worry, whatever you can't eat, we'll box up and take home."

They stared into each other for a moment. She was so freaking beautiful. If she let him, he would buy her pie every day. A different flavor for each day of the week. Who was he kidding? He'd do much more than buy her a slice of pie every day if she agreed to be his. He'd get her whatever the hell she wanted, whenever she wanted.

Suddenly, she drew her hand back. "Oh, I forgot. I got you something." She started routing through her bag and pulled out a plain white box. She then proceeded to slide it across the wooden tabletop. "It's a housewarming present."

"You didn't have to get me anything, doll. I haven't even moved in yet."

Curiosity won out. Quickly. And he tore open the cardboard box like a kid at Christmas. He pulled at the object until it was completely out, and just stared. Dumbfounded. A sudden clog of emotion filled his throat. When he didn't say anything, Summer filled the silence.

"Uh, it's a cuckoo clock. Like when you were little. I remember you telling me about the one your mom had that used to drive your dad crazy, and I saw this ... and, uh ... I thought that uh ... if you don't like it, I can take it back. I got it at the gift shop down the road ... I didn't get a gift receipt ... but I'm sure Bob won't mind exchanging it for something else."

Teddy finally looked up to see the concern on her pretty face. He wanted to fix that. Immediately. But the only words he seemed able to choke out were, "You remembered that?"

"I remember everything, Teddy." Her serious expression hit him hard. Because this was serious. He was seriously gone for this woman.

"Thank you, doll. This means ... this means a hell of a whole lot. More than you know."

He was pleased to see her shoulders sag a little. Less worried and more relaxed as she reached across the table and took hold of his hand again. Teddy looked down at her small hand interlaced with his much bigger one and smiled. This was right. She was right. And his goddamn sister was right. He'd been in love with Summer Willis a long ass time. This time though, there was no way in hell he was going to let her go.

CHAPTER TEN

Something was up with Teddy. He'd been acting weird ever since she'd given him the cuckoo clock. At first, when he didn't say anything, she was worried she'd overstepped. The memory of his mom's clock was a personal one that he'd shared with her a long time ago.

She still remembered that night. It was burned into her memory. It must have been only a year after his parents' car accident. They were thirteen. She'd found him in their spot. Crying. Listing the silly things he missed about them had been her idea. It was supposed to help.

Going by Teddy's reaction, she hadn't crossed any boundaries with the gift. Thank God. But he was still acting strange. Every time she looked over at him, he was staring at her. He didn't even pretend to look away when she caught him, like a normal person. And he had this ridiculously intense expression on his face. It was making her squirm. She didn't know where to look or what to do. And every time she caught sight of those flaming eyes, she seemed to melt under the heat.

"I talked to my buddy Tyler the other night," Teddy announced as they continued their ride across Moonrock's sun-soaked fields. "He wants to meet you."

"Okay. I have questions. Who is Tyler? Where does he live? What did you tell him about me? And when do I get to meet him?"

Teddy's hearty laugh warmed her belly. "Navy. We were on the same team together. We were buddies before though, known him almost ten years. Remember I told you I was a POW? Well, Tyler was the other survivor. Only he had worse injuries than me."

"Oh," was the only reply Summer could manage as her mouth suddenly went dry.

"Yeah. He had an infection in one of his legs … they had to amputate. He has a prosthetic now. He's still in California, so I don't see him much, but I check in every month, make sure he's okay. He took the loss …" Teddy paused to take a deep breath. "Let's just say he didn't adjust well. And what with losing two of our teammates as well …" His words trailed off as he stared into the distance. She realized pretty quickly that she needed to say something other than *oh*.

"I'm sorry."

Really? That's the best you could do?

Teddy pulled on the reigns of his chocolate-colored mare and came to a halt. Summer followed suit and came to a stop next to him. The air was still thick with emotion. As he turned to face her, she could feel herself holding her breath.

"I've never really spoken to anyone about what happened over there. Not to anyone who isn't a Navy-issued psychiatrist anyway. Not even to Tyler." Teddy's eyes were boring into her now, and she couldn't look away if her life depended on it. "But I want you to know. I want to tell you."

"Whatever you want to tell me, Teddy … you can. But there's no rush. I know it's hard for you. And I know it's not going to be a pretty story. Whenever you're ready … I'll be here."

What she really wanted was to hear it all. Now. She had

ever since he'd told her he was captured. The bad, the ugly, the damn-right scary. Then she wanted to comfort him. Hold him. Kiss him. Tell him everything was going to be all right. But despite his declaration, deep down she knew he wasn't ready yet. If he hadn't even talked to Tyler about what went down, it meant he'd been burying this stuff for a long time. And it was bad. Really bad. Bad enough to make him change his mind about being a SEAL.

"I really wanna kiss you right now." The corner of his mouth tilted up. "I really didn't think this whole horse-riding date through, huh?"

"How 'bout we head back? Then … we can make out in your truck." She shot him a wink.

That panty-melting smile grew wider. "Let's go."

"Race you?" Teddy immediately took off, choosing a non-verbal reply to her challenge. She made sure to shout after him as she kicked Blaze's side. "Cheater!"

***

Two weeks after their Moonrock ride and subsequent make-out session, Summer had been on four more dates with Teddy. Their third date had been the typical dinner and a movie. For their fourth date he'd taken her to see some live music in the next town over. On their fifth date they hung out at her place and got takeout. And, finally, their sixth date consisted of another trip to Teddy's cabin, this time during the day. Things seemed to be going well. Kind of.

There were no problems per se. Every time she saw Teddy, whether it was on a date or at work, they joked, laughed, and they kissed like horny teenagers. But that was it. No groping. No overnight stays. And definitely no hanky-panky. He hadn't even hinted that he wanted said hanky-panky. She was starting to get a complex.

Stop being paranoid. He just wants to take it slow.

That was probably it. Not every man wanted to jump

straight into bed. That sounded possible. Kind of.

"We should get a stripper," Laney chirped, downing the remnants of her second glass of wine. "Or go to one of those strip shows. We can get Ivy a lap dance!"

Ivy giggled while Summer frowned. This wasn't a good idea. Laney was a liability. She'd crashed her and Ivy's bachelorette party planning session about an hour ago, claiming she needed an alcoholic break from her kids. Summer should have known as soon as she waltzed into Mickey's that things were going to go downhill. Fast. At least Teddy wasn't working today. Distracting her.

But he's having a grand old time distracting you in your head.

Shaking away those thoughts, Summer tried her best to concentrate on one disaster at a time. "No strippers, Lanes. I'm under strict orders from her fiancé that no naked males are to go anywhere near her."

Ivy giggled even harder. "Yeah, Ace would lose his mind. He actually growled at Luke the other day when he came over to check on one of the horses."

"Hot Luke? The vet?" Laney asked.

"Yup. He thinks Luke is into me. Supposedly he looks at me too long and he flashes too much teeth when he smiles at me. Honestly, the man can be ridiculous sometimes. Poor Luke though. Getting growled at. Even if it was kinda funny to witness."

Summer's frown cracked at the image of Ace growling at Luke. Ace was a big softie when it came to Ivy, but to anyone else she could see how he might come across as quite intimidating.

As Ivy and Laney continued to discuss Luke, Summer's phone vibrated in her pocket. She pulled it out only to see Teddy's name flash on the screen. What had she been saying about distractions?

Teddy: *Dinner tonight at my place?*

Summer: *What we having?*

Teddy: *It's a surprise. How's the bachelorette planning going?*

Summer: *Laney suggested strippers. Interested in earning a few* *extra bucks?*

Teddy: *Fuck no. Private shows only.*

Summer: *How does one go about booking a private show? Asking for a friend.*

Teddy: *It involves asking me nicely. Preferably naked.*

Summer almost choked on her tongue. That conversation took a turn. A very interesting one. Maybe he was after some hanky-panky after all.

"Are you blushing?" Laney grinned her way.

"Uh, no, it's just hot in here. Must be the wine."

"Oh yeah, who you texting?"

Damn her friend. Damn her to hell. "No one." She shot Laney a *drop it* look that she'd perfected over years of friendship.

"Oh my god, you're texting my brother, aren't you?" Ivy chimed in.

Fuck my life.

"Anyway ... back to the party. No strippers. How do you guys feel about karaoke?" Summer ignored the phone in her hand, which was currently buzzing.

"Are you gonna get that?" Laney asked, smirking at Summer's phone.

"Oh, leave her alone," Ivy beamed, "her and Teddy are still in the early phases of dating. You remember how it was with Max, right? All hot and heavy. Wondering what each other are doing every second of the day. I think it's cute."

"So you don't mind her sexting your brother then?" Laney helpfully added.

"I am not sexting Teddy!" Summer screeched. Just a little too loud. Heads seemed to swivel, and another round of laughter erupted from both her friends.

After attempting her best scowl, she ignored the giggling women and turned her attention back to her messages.

Teddy: *Too soon?*

Teddy: *Summer?*

Teddy: *I'm sorry. I was joking. All my clothes will be staying firmly in place tonight. Promise.*

Shoot. He was panicking because she hadn't answered. And apparently trying to move their relationship backward.

Summer: *Sorry. Planning emergency. I hope you're joking about your clothes staying on. What happened to my private show?*

Teddy: *Phew. I thought I scared you off. You really want a private show?*

Summer: *No, you didn't, and yes, I do :)*

Teddy: *You gonna ask nicely?*

Summer: *I'm always nice!*

Teddy: *Naked?*

Summer: *Well, I've heard that's the only way to book.*

Teddy: *How soon can you come over?*

This time she did take a moment to laugh. And squirm. She checked the time. Okay, she needed to wrap up this meeting and go shave. She had a date with a hot man. A naked date.

***

Summer tried once again to check her unease and knocked on Teddy's apartment door. She'd already given herself a good talking to on her way over. Shaved, showered, and in her good underwear that matched and everything, she really shouldn't be nervous. Yet, she was pretty sure she was shaking.

This is Teddy. My Teddy. I've wanted this since forever.

Maybe that was the problem though. She'd built this moment up in her head since she was twelve years old. Well, maybe sixteen years old. At twelve, she just wanted to hold his hand. What if it didn't live up to her expectations? What if she didn't live up to his?

No pressure then.

Teddy swung open the door and she watched as his face flicked from unadulterated lust to sudden concern. Damnit. She was doing a piss-poor job of hiding her nerves. When did she become so transparent?

"What's wrong, doll? Jesus, you're trembling." He

gathered her into his big, strong arms and held her close.

Resting her head against his shoulder, she relaxed into him. This felt better. This felt right. "It's silly. I feel silly now. I'm fine. Honestly."

"Talk to me, doll." He didn't let her go, just pulled her along with him as he moved them back inside the apartment and shut the door.

Taking in a deep breath, she let the musky scent of his cologne and soap soothe her. "I'm nervous."

Loosening his arms, he drew back just enough to tilt her face up and aim that green-eyed gaze at her. "Nothing needs to happen tonight. This goes at your pace, okay? I've waited a fucking lifetime to be with you, Summer. Another few weeks, months, hell … even another year doesn't mean jack. I'll wait however long you want."

I've waited a lifetime to be with you too.

That was the thing about Teddy. He always knew what to say. How to put her at ease and make her feel safe. Suddenly, she didn't feel so afraid anymore. So what if tonight wasn't perfect? If *she* wasn't perfect. This was right. He was right. Nothing else mattered.

Summer rose onto her tiptoes and zeroed in on Teddy's lips. Her heart was thumping its way out of her ribcage, but at least she was no longer shaking. As their mouths met, she nipped at his lower lip and pried him open. Once her tongue swept inside, the kiss turned urgent as they swallowed each other's moans.

Curling her hands around his neck, she tugged his head down further so she could get deeper. Nerves be damned, she wanted more. She wanted all of him.

Teddy's hands freely wandered. They gently brushed down her back, one stopping to grip her waist while the other traveled further south and landed on her ass. His strong grip only spurred her on more. Untangling one of her own hands, she let her fingers trail between them all the way down to the hem of his shirt. Taking the hint, Teddy helped her tug the material up and all the way over his head.

"Are you sure?" His breathless voice shot liquid heat right through her.

Her eyes went straight to his bare chest. So this was what a shirtless Teddy looked like. Glorious. Muscles over muscles speckled with a dusting of dark hair. Black ink traveled all the way up his arm, across his collarbone, and came to rest over his heart.

Holy mother of shitballs. He's a work of art. A sexy-as-hell work of art.

"Doll?" Teddy's deep rumble sent a shiver down her spine.

She tore her eyes away from that illustrious V-shaped muscle and met his fiery stare. "I'm sure, Teddy. I want you."

As soon as the last word was out, his mouth crashed back down onto hers. Gasping in shock, he took advantage and plunged his tongue inside. Hungry didn't even begin to cover the kiss he bestowed on her. Ravenous. Greedy. Starving. Was more like it.

Her top was next to be pushed up, and she lost his lips as it was torn over her head and tossed aside. Lucky for her, he was back on her seconds later, latching onto that sweet spot between her neck and shoulder. Launching a frenzied attack on her senses, he sucked, scraped, and soothed until she was sure her brain cells would never recover.

Both his hands now gripped her ass. "Be sure, doll, 'cause after we do this, there's no turning back. You'll be mine, Summer. *Mine*. And I don't plan on letting you go."

"I've always been yours, Teddy. Always." She panted, trying desperately to catch her breath.

The grip on her butt tightened until she was airborne. Getting with the program, she held onto Teddy's shoulders and wrapped her legs around his hips. It was her turn to let her mouth explore as he walked them to the bedroom. Dragging her lips across his throat, she felt herself smile when a guttural groan ripped right through him and vibrated against her core.

"You know, when you say shit like that to me, doll, it makes me wanna tie you to my goddamn bed and do wicked … wicked things to you."

"Fine by me."

Summer stifled a giggle as her words were met with a thunderous roar. Or was it a growl? Whatever it was, it was hot.

After being unceremoniously dropped onto the bed, she leaned on her elbows and got her first look at the beast she'd unleashed. Teddy stood at the foot of the bed, jaw clenched, chest heaving. He was clearly on the verge of losing all control. And she couldn't wait to witness what that looked like.

"Clothes off," was all he said as he unclasped his belt.

Who was she to deny him?

CHAPTER ELEVEN

Teddy let out a content sigh as Summer continued to trace the tattoo across his chest. They never made it to dinner, not that he was complaining. He'd take Summer in his arms over food any day of the week.

"I never realized this was a tree. I always thought the strokes on your arm were like tribal patterns or something, like on the other arm … I never would've guessed they were tree roots. It makes sense now though."

The tattoo she was talking about was all black ink. The tree roots started on his forearm and worked their way up until they transformed into a thick trunk. Branches began to spread over his bicep, collarbone, and across his chest, with black birds emerging from the offshoots over his heart.

"Is that your nice way of saying it looks crap?" Teddy chuckled. Summer was never very subtle.

"No!" She jerked in his arms and shot up to face him, her hand still resting against his bare chest. "It's beautiful, Teddy. Really beautiful."

She was wrong. She was the only beautiful thing in the room. Her silky blonde hair was all mussed and hung in all different directions. Green flecks peeked through heavy eyelids. And her pretty pink lips were still swollen from hours of kissing.

Gently tugging her back down, she came willingly until her head was back on his shoulder. "Thank you, doll. I got this one when I left the Navy. See the birds that emerge from the tree?" He felt her nod against him. "Two are for my parents ... the other two are for Mason and Carter. My teammates."

"The ones you lost." It wasn't a question, but he answered regardless.

"Yeah. The ones I lost."

"I'm sorry," she whispered, "tell me about them. What were they like?"

Teddy dropped a kiss onto her hair. "They were good guys. Mason was a bit of a joker. Used to drive me and Ty crazy with his pranks. They were non-stop. This one time in Germany, he placed a load of bubble wrap under the bathmats in our hotel room. Of course we'd been out drinking the night before. The morning after, I go into the bathroom to brush my teeth and I swear to God I almost had a heart attack when the loudest goddamn pop had me ducking for cover." A smile broke out as he remembered how hard Mason had laughed when he'd found him laid out on the floor of the bathroom.

"And Carter?"

"Carter was more reserved. The strong and silent type I guess. From what he told me, he had it rough as a kid. He grew up in foster care and was passed around a lot. He didn't say much, but when he did ... people listened."

Summer snuggled deeper into the crook of his arm, distracting him momentarily from the pang of grief that was now making his chest feel tight.

"I wish I could've met them."

"Me too, doll, me too."

Teddy ran his fingers up and down the smooth skin on Summer's back as they fell into a comfortable silence. Thoughts of Mason and Carter eventually subsided, and for the first time in a long time, he felt at peace.

After a while he heard Summer's breathing slow and a cute little snore escape her lips. He felt like he should pinch himself to check that this was real. His dream woman was asleep in his arms. In his bed. Naked. Goddamn, he was one lucky man.

"Sweet dreams, Summer." He dropped a kiss onto her forehead and whispered, "I love you," into the night.

***

"What you doing here, man?" Ace casually leaned against the wooden doorframe, narrowed blue eyes boring into Teddy and a hint of confusion creasing the mottled skin on one side of his face.

"Summer sent me." Teddy gestured to the bed of his truck behind him. "I got some decking for the yard." When his soon-to-be brother-in-law's expression still looked perplexed, he continued. "For the platform, man. Y'know, for the ceremony? So you can marry my sister?"

"Oh shit," he exclaimed, immediately straightening.

"Yeah. Oh shit. You gonna help me unload?"

With a nod, Ace was off the porch and circling the truck. They worked together to unload and carry everything around to the backyard.

This was not how Teddy imagined spending his day off. In between work and Summer playing wedding planner, the only time they'd spent together this past week had been at night. In bed. Not that having Summer in his bed every night wasn't a good time. It was. A very good time. But he wanted more. Now that they'd taken things to the next level physically, he wanted to make sure they were on the same page emotionally.

Despite the lack of time they'd spent together, he could tell something was going on with her, and it was making him uneasy. He was hoping to talk to her properly today, but then he'd been summoned here. Maybe she was already aware that he was incapable of denying her? If not, it was only a matter of time. So here he was. Spending the day with Ace. Building a freaking stage.

Who are you kidding? You'd build a million stages for her if it made her happy.

After settling on a place to set up the decking, they got to work building a frame. They worked together quickly and quietly, only stopping to check on each other's progress. So, he was surprised an hour in when Ace asked out of the blue how things were going with Summer.

"Good." Teddy grunted, ignoring the churning in his gut. Things were good, right? They were more than compatible in the bedroom. And outside of it, everything was just so easy.

So why are you desperate to have a heart-to-heart with her about your feelings?

"You sure about that?"

Teddy looked up to see Ace wiping sweat from his brow as he lowered his power drill.

"What's that supposed to mean?"

Ace took his time studying him before replying. "It means you don't sound so sure about that."

Teddy let out a sigh and heaved himself up. "Is this what we're doing now … sharing? You wanna braid my hair too?"

"Fuck off, Teddy, you don't have to be an asshole."

As he watched his sister's fiancé shake his head in exasperation, Teddy blew out a long breath. Great. Now he felt guilty. Summer was making him soft.

"Look, man, I'm sorry." Ace went from pissed off to suspicious as Teddy spoke. "I didn't get much sleep last night … I swear to God, man, wipe that look off your face right fucking now, or I'll wipe it off for you!"

Ace threw up his hands defensively. "Whoa, whoa, whoa! Cool it, man. I didn't say jackshit."

"Don't even pretend you weren't about to. Your eyebrows practically shot up to your hairline the moment I mentioned not getting enough sleep."

"So now you're the eyebrow police, dude?"

Teddy felt his lips twitch, but he refused to allow a smile to crack. "We're not on a dude basis yet."

"Oh no?" Ace didn't seem to have the same trouble as he did flashing his pearly whites. "How about *brother?* After all, in just one short week that's what we'll be." He was enjoying this way too much.

"I really fucking hate you."

"Has anyone ever told you that you swear like a sailor?" Ace doubled over laughing at his own joke.

Teddy prayed for patience. He couldn't punch the man in the face. Could he?

Ivy will give you so much shit if you ruin her wedding pictures.

He was obviously thinking too long. He hadn't even noticed that Ace had stopped laughing until that smarmy Southern drawl was back and polluting his ears once again.

"Come on, Teddy. You gonna tell me what's going on with you? You're even more ornery than usual. Or ... shall I go get your sister and have her drag it out of you?"

Fucking Ace.

Teddy didn't even know how to reply. It was true. He wasn't acting like a man in love. And he was. He got the girl. Finally. But that niggling feeling making the hairs on the back of his neck prick up was mocking him. Something was wrong. He could feel it.

Over the years, he'd learned to trust his gut. It had kept him alive on more than one occasion during his time in the Navy. But this wasn't a mission. This was a relationship. And he had no idea what he was doing.

Teddy used his sleeve to swat the sweat trickling down his face. "Fine," he huffed. "I think something's up with Summer, but I don't know what. I don't know if it's something I've done or said or didn't do. I'm clueless. Happy?"

"That's it?"

Teddy looked up to find Ace frowning at him. "What do you mean *that's it?*" Did the man not hear him say he was clueless?

"Well, brother, there's this thing in relationships called communication. In case you didn't know … that means talking."

Yep, decision made. Teddy was definitely going to punch Ace. Wedding photos be damned.

"Have you tried asking her what's wrong?"

What was Teddy thinking going to this clown for relationship advice?

He's the one getting married.

"Of course I've asked her; I'm not a complete fucking idiot." Teddy scoffed. "Every time I ask her if she's okay, she tells me she's fine."

It was Ace's turn to sigh. "Look. Before you ask her again … maybe you could try opening up to her first? If she knows where your head's at, maybe she'll be more comfortable telling you what's going on with her."

Huh. That sort of made sense.

"That's what you did with my sister, huh?"

"Yup. And look at me now." Ace's lopsided grin was back. "Bona fide relationship expert. Just call me Dr. Love."

This time Teddy did laugh right along with Ace. Maybe having him as a brother wouldn't be so bad after all.

***

Teddy muted the television and tugged Summer closer to him on the couch. Not that they weren't close already. He just needed to get rid of that pesky air between their bodies.

"Everything okay?" Summer kept her head against his chest but tilted upward until he was looking into those hypnotic eyes.

"Yeah, doll, I just thought we'd talk for a bit."

Summer stiffened in his arms and dropped her head again. That was not a good sign.

Letting his fingers gently trail up and down her spine, he waited until she'd relaxed back into him before he continued. "Remember when I told you I wanted you to know what happened to me?"

"Yeah."

"Well, I'm ready to tell you." Summer shifted until her hand came to rest over his heart. "Is that okay?"

Her eyes met his once again with another slight tilt to her face. "I want to know whatever you want to tell me. I can handle it. I promise."

Teddy nodded and ushered her to return to her previous position. "I was in Iraq. On a mission. It all happened really fast. We were scoping out the area one minute and being ambushed the next." He took a moment to clear his throat. "When I woke up, I was chained up. Alone. Well, not for long. I'm not gonna go into details of what they did to me— you've already seen the scars." And kissed every single one of them. Just remembering her lips on him gave him the strength he needed to let the memories creep back in. "I wasn't in great shape, but I held up. The training I underwent prepared me for most of it." Mason and Carter's faces flashed before him, triggering the familiar twist in his stomach.

"But not all of it," Summer correctly surmised.

"No. Not all of it." He swallowed down the bile now rising up his throat. He knew he needed to say it out loud. Rip off the Band-Aid. "One of the tactics they used was to bring another teammate in when they …" Tortured us. That, he didn't need to say. She got the drift. "They brought Mason into my cell. Did the same shit to him they'd been doing to me and made me watch." Teddy could hear Summer's sharp inhale. She probably knew what was coming. Regardless, he needed to say it out loud. "They obviously weren't getting the reactions they wanted from us. A couple of days in, they decided to take it further."

"They killed him, didn't they?" Summer whispered into his chest. "In front of you."

"Yeah, doll. They did." His vision blurred as tears filled his eyes. But the image of Mason's last breath was still crystal clear. Forever ingrained in his soul.

"And Carter?"

"Thrown in with Tyler." Teddy's throat tightened. "From what Ty said, the same thing went down."

They both fell silent. Long enough for Teddy to begin second-guessing himself. He did the right thing by telling her, right? If they were going to be together, he owed her the truth. Owed her an explanation as to why he left. Why he sometimes woke up in the middle of the night drenched in sweat. Why he was so broken.

All of a sudden, Summer was on the move, crawling onto his lap and positioning her knees on either side of him. Resting her forehead against his, she let her hands travel down his torso, lightly trailing her fingers over him in soothing motions.

"I'm so, so sorry." Her soft, angelic voice was like a balm he never knew he needed. Until now.

Matching tears trickled down her cheeks and merged with his own as her salty lips pressed against his. Teddy breathed her in and allowed the vanilla-scented fumes to scramble his senses. Raw need ripped through him. He was a dying man, and she was the only cure.

Taking control, he nibbled on her lower lip until she parted for him. Once she was open, he took what he wanted. Needed. Their tongues danced in a sensuous rhythm to each other's moans, sucking and tasting until the rest of his body began to burn.

He brought his hands up to encircle her delicate face. In contrast to the urgency of their kiss, his thumbs moved lightly across her cheeks. Stroking. Caressing. Swiping away the wet, hot grief that still clung to them both.

Untangling his tongue, he ran his lips along the curve of her jaw. Shifting his hands further back into the silky strands of her hair, he followed the line all the way up to the sensitive shell of her ear. Before he even spoke, he felt her tremble beneath his touch.

"I need you, baby." He let his hot breath hover before

tasting every goosebump that broke out in its wake.

Once he reached the nape of her neck, he bit down, eliciting a whimper that had fire shooting through his veins. Sucking on the same spot, she began to rock on his lap. This is what he needed. The relief he had been searching for. Only she could give it to him. Summer. His Summer.

CHAPTER TWELVE

Summer couldn't sleep. It must have been at least an hour since Teddy's breath had evened out and he'd fallen asleep on his back. Her eyes hadn't left him the whole time. She was laying on her side, staring at him. Like a weirdo.

Hearing about his time as a POW had almost broken her. Just the thought of him being physically hurt made her want to hurl, but the mental torture he endured, that was like a dagger to her heart.

"You gonna stare at me all night, doll, or you gonna tell me what's going on in that beautiful head of yours?" Teddy's voice was low and sleep-roughened. Yet still so very sexy.

Summer narrowed her eyes. Surely he hadn't been faking being asleep. "You were sleeping," she lamely stated.

"What's going on, dollface?"

"What makes you think something is going on?"

Teddy rolled onto his side until they were face to face. "Summer. Baby. I know you, remember? You've not been yourself since I took you to bed. A week ago. Now, either you're severely disappointed by my equipment and how I use it … or something else is going on with you. Which is it?"

She shot up off her pillow. "What? No! I'm not disappointed! It's not that!" How could he even think that?

The smug smirk he flung her way as he tugged her back down said it all. He didn't think that. He'd played her. Damn him.

"Bastard," she mumbled, ignoring Teddy's throaty chuckle.

As soon as his laugh subsided, she instantly felt the air thicken. His hand was on her face a second later, tilting it up to meet his gaze. "Talk to me, doll. Please."

Her heart rate picked up, and she could no longer look him in the eye. Instead, she dropped her gaze to his chest and began to play with his dark hair. Neither of them spoke for several minutes. It was like he knew she was trying to get her thoughts in order, and he was giving her time.

Eventually she blurted out the truth. Not so eloquently. "I'm scared."

"Of what?"

"Of this. Of us." She let out a slow breath, realizing how shaky her voice was. "I don't know how to do this. How to be in a healthy relationship. How to just be … happy."

Teddy had moved closer. His hand was resting on her hip one minute and pulling her into him the next. Accepting his comfort, she let her head rest in the crook of his neck as he stroked her side. "It's okay; it's okay. Explain it to me, doll. Talk me through it."

She swallowed down the lump in her throat. Thank God her face was hidden, and Teddy couldn't see her now-burning cheeks. "It's embarrassing …" She paused and let the soothing motion of his fingers give her strength. "I haven't … I don't have much experience when it comes to guys."

She felt Teddy's body tense. She was once again glad that he couldn't see her face. If she wanted to get through this, she needed to keep her attention as far from those green flames as possible.

"We never really talked about what happened when we

… when we were younger. But, um, you, uh … you weren't the only one who was a virgin when you left for the Navy." She could feel his heart thumping against her bare chest. She could swear that it had grown faster. "I guess I … I, uh, I always thought you'd be my first."

A tortured groan echoed around the quiet room, followed by a string of expletives. She waited for him to stop, burying her head farther into his neck.

When he'd finally finished cursing a blue streak, she steeled herself. She'd come this far. No point turning back now.

"Before you, I'd only ever been in two relationships. Colt … and Ben."

"Jesus Christ, Summer. I-I … that's …"

"Pathetic," she finished his sentence for him. "I know. I'm a thirty-four-year-old woman for God's sake, trust me I know that I'm—"

Before she could finish, she was flipped onto her back. Her hands pinned on either side of her head as Teddy loomed over her. Even in the darkness she could see that his eyes were blazing.

"Call yourself pathetic one more time, Summer, and I'll spank that pretty little butt of yours until you're walking around with my handprints on it."

"Uh …" She stopped. She had no idea what to say. Yes, please?

"Let me get this straight, doll. You've only ever been with two men?"

"Um … and you … so, uh, three, technically."

More curses trickled out. Each one more creative than the last. "If I didn't already hate that motherfucker Colt, I sure as shit do now. And that asshole Ben. Fuck. It's my fault. All of it."

"What?"

"It's my fault, baby. If I'd have just manned up all those years ago and told you how I felt …"

She jiggled her hands until they were free from his grasp

and cradled his face. She could clearly see the regret swimming in the creases around his temple. She wanted to kiss it away.

"Don't. Don't do that. We're here now, aren't we? We found each other again. That's all that matters." She lifted until her lips brushed his forehead and continued her assault until his whole face had been covered in kisses. "I just needed you to know. I needed you to understand why I might be bad at this. Why I'm probably gonna fuck up." This time she pressed a kiss to his lips and inhaled his musky scent.

He lowered his forehead to hers. The move pushed her back onto the pillow. "I want to give you everything, doll. You know that, right?" He didn't wait for her to reply. "I wanna show you what a relationship is supposed to be like. How you're meant to be treated. How you're supposed to be loved. Everything you've never had. And I swear to God, that's what I'm gonna strive to do. Every. Single. Day."

Holy shit. Did he just say loved? No. He can't have meant it like that. Not yet. It's too soon. See? This just proves how much I suck at this!

She was still trying to think of a reply that wasn't "okay" when he continued to blow her mind. "But, baby, there's something you should know too. Your two relationships … well, that's two more than me. I'm flying fucking blind here. Literally. You're scared you're gonna fuck this up? Well, I'm fucking terrified."

Oh my God. Seriously?

How was it possible that this beautiful man had never been in a relationship before? As if reading her mind, she didn't need to wait too long for an answer.

"Don't get me wrong, doll, I've had my fair share of encounters. Casual ones. But relationships? I've got zero experience. Seeing as we're laying all our cards on the table tonight …" He drew up slightly so he could capture her eyes, her pulse immediately quickened when she got a glimpse of the intensity in his expression. "No one was you,

Summer. Not one single person came close."

Her chest tightened. It was suddenly hard to breathe. Hard to think. And evidently too hard to speak as well because all she managed to say in reply was, "Teddy".

"What was the point in dating when I knew I wouldn't ... *couldn't* ever feel for anyone what I felt for you?"

She hadn't even noticed she'd sprung a leak until tears spilled over her cheeks, dampening her ears. Overwhelmed didn't even begin to cover how she was feeling. The last thing she wanted was to dwell on the past, but now all she could think about was what if. They'd wasted so much time.

"Kiss me," she whispered, "make me yours."

A growl erupted before his mouth claimed hers. If she thought his kisses had felt possessive before, she'd had no damn clue. As he devoured and tasted every inch of her, contentment settled over her. She felt owned. Worshipped. Loved. She was his and he was hers. Fucking finally.

***

Summer had spent the past few days practically glued to Teddy's hip. She never really considered herself clingy in a relationship. Or in need of any sort of validation. If anything, past boyfriends—well, Colt and Ben—had accused her of being distant. Too independent. They'd even gone as far as to say she was cold. So, the revelation that she wanted to spend every free minute she had wrapped up in Teddy had surprised even her.

She certainly wasn't cold with him either. If anything, it was the opposite. They couldn't stop touching each other. Much to the dismay of everyone around them. Kelly had spent most of last night's shift making vomiting sounds every time she caught them making out.

This was what happiness felt like. This was what being in love felt like.

Yes. Love. Sickeningly happy, cringe-inducing, epic love. In all its glory. The realization might have only come after they'd shared, but that wasn't when she'd fallen in love with him. Their love had spanned decades. He had always been the one who got away. An unrequited love that wasn't so unrequited anymore.

When did I get so sappy?

Tonight, she'd dragged her sappy ass to the next town over for Ivy's bachelorette party. As Mickey's was the only bar in Bluestone, they'd had to venture out to Splitrock, the next town over, so the husbands of the women didn't crash the party. It would appear that they were all just as possessive as Teddy and didn't like the idea of their women getting tipsy when there were other men nearby.

The whole possessive thing was new to Summer. At first she thought Teddy was being controlling, which pissed her right off. And she had no problem telling him so. She'd had enough of controlling assholes. But as soon as they'd talked about it and he'd explained the last thing he wanted to do was control her, she got it. It stemmed from concern. Her safety. Nothing else. Well, possibly a little caveman jealousy too, going by his reaction to her dress tonight.

"Make room for the shots, ladies!" Alice piped as a tray full of dark liquid came into view.

"Please tell me those aren't whiskey shots, Ali." Her sister, Lily, grimaced.

"As if there's any other kind of shot, Lilypad." Mirth danced in Alice's pretty blue eyes.

Summer had to admit, she loved these women. They'd welcomed her and Laney into their fold with open arms. And they were funny as hell.

Ivy, Lily, Sam, and Laney all stared at the shot glasses Alice placed in front of each of them. Summer was the first to throw it back and wince at the burn it left in its wake. She might as well start as she meant to go on.

"Well damn," Alice yelled over the country music blasting in the background, "my kinda woman!" She brought her own shot glass to her lips and knocked it back.

"I can't drink that, Ali." Lily pushed her shot toward her

sister.

"And why is that, Lilypad?" She had a feeling that Alice already knew the answer. Even Summer was pretty sure she could guess.

Lily shook her head in exasperation. "Okay, okay. I was planning on saving this until *after* the wedding, but since my little sister is being her usual annoying self, I guess that's not gonna happen. I can't drink these nasty-looking shots because … I'm pregnant. Again."

Instead of the usual congratulations, the women around the table all burst into a fit of laughter. Sam even began to double over. Laney and Summer were the only ones not privy to the joke and exchanged a baffled look.

"Is someone going to tell me what you're all laughing about?" Lily demanded.

Ivy was the first woman to compose herself, but her playful smile remained in place. "I'm sorry, Lily. It's just we already knew. We had a bet going on to see how long it took you to tell us … and Ali here had her money on tonight. We really shoulda known she was gonna trick you into telling us!"

"You knew? You all knew?!" Lily screeched. "And, Ali, what the hell are you doing making bets when I told you a month ago that I was pregnant?"

Alice managed to compose herself long enough to reply, "Well, technically, the bet was about when you were going to announce it to everyone, not just to me."

"Is someone gonna tell me how you all knew?"

Sam, Jake's sister, was the only one brave enough to break the news. "I'm sorry, Lily, but you know my brother is really bad at keeping secrets. Like, really bad. He let it slip to Brady and Duke a couple of months ago. And, well, the rest is history."

Attempting to ease the scowl forming across Lily's delicate, porcelain features, Summer raised her hand. "Uh, I didn't know. Nor did Laney." She flashed the woman her warmest smile. "Congratulations, you and Jake must be really excited."

Laney was quick to add her own well-wishes too. Effectively deflating any tension.

Lily revealing pregnancy number two was as dramatic as it got. The rest of the night was spent drinking way too many shots and lots of line dancing.

Taking a break from the action on the dance floor, Summer returned to the table, which Lily was currently guarding. Poor woman had been fending off suitors all night. Not that she could blame the male population of Splitrock for giving it their best shot. Lily was stunning. Her long hair was golden with a natural wave. And her eyes were even greener than Teddy's. Add in a slamming body and a friendly smile, she was basically whatever catnip was to cats but for men.

"How you holding up?" Summer jumped onto the blue cushioned booth seat next to Lily.

"Well, I have video evidence of a very drunk Ali trying to line dance to "Cotton Eye Joe" … so all in all, it's a good night." She ended with a wink.

Summer let out a chuckle. "You two are just as bad as each other."

"You got any siblings?"

"Nah. I was enough of a handful for my parents, at least that's what they told me." Many, many times. Summer was used to being the ultimate disappointment. She honestly assumed that her parents stopped with her because they were mortified by the idea of having another child turn out the same way.

When it came to Mr. and Mrs. Willis, nothing Summer did was ever good enough. Her grades, her hobbies, her friends. The most important thing to her parents was what other people thought. So when Summer refused to go to college, that was the final straw. Heaven forbid she forgo a college education and travel around the world instead. Apparently only stoner hippies wanting to bring shame on the family did something so shocking.

"Are your parents still in Bluestone?"

"Nope. Florida. They moved over there a while ago." To get away from all that shame Summer assumed.

"I'm guessing you guys aren't close?"

"That obvious?" Summer's attempt at breezy fell short. Really short. She didn't like to think about her parents, let alone talk about them. Throw alcohol into the mix and let's just say she was pretty fricking close to losing her buzz.

"Kinda, honey, but we don't have to talk about it if you don't want to. I know how it is. I'm kinda an expert when it comes to shitshow families."

"Yeah?"

"Oh yeah. So, if you ever wanna compare notes … you have my number."

"I just might take you up on that," before Summer could say anything more, their attention shot to the stage.

"Ladies and gentlemen, it's that time of the night! Kicking off this evening's karaoke is the lovely Alice Mitchell from Bluestone County."

Cheers and whoops filled the bar, the loudest being from Laney, Sam, and Ivy, who were hollering from the dance floor as Alice jumped on stage.

Looks like Summer had been wrong. The party was only just beginning.

CHAPTER THIRTEEN

Teddy stood by the entrance. Arms crossed. Brow crinkled. And lips twitching. As he watched an extremely drunk Summer try her hand at karaoke. This time it was piña coladas that she was singing about.

Why was she always singing about drinks? And why the heck had he let her leave the house in that goddamn dress? If that tiny piece of blue polyester rose any higher, he was ready to storm the stage and carry her home. Caveman style.

Whoops and cheers from the male punters had Teddy's blood pressure rising and his fists clenching.

"Easy, man." Jake clapped his shoulder. "We're here to take our women home … not take out every drunk dude in the bar."

Teddy rolled his shoulders, focusing solely on Summer and how happy she looked. So carefree. And radiant.

That'll probably be the whiskey shots if I know my girl.

"Fine. Let's get to it then, before I change my mind." He grunted as he started to stalk toward the corner table where the rest of the women were gathered.

He'd had to fend off Brady, Duke, and Ace for the chance to pick up the women tonight, all of who were anxious to see their other halves. Everyone knew by now that Lily was pregnant, so Jake had automatically been picked as one of the designated drivers. Teddy, though, had found himself offering free drinks at Mickey's for his chance to pick up Summer. And not just because she was hilarious after a couple of whiskey shots, no, it was more than that. He missed her. Badly. Even though it had only been a few hours since he'd seen her.

You've got it really bad, man.

And didn't he know it. Feeling actual physical pain being away from Summer was a new, worrying, and scary development that he hadn't had time yet to decipher.

"Ladies," Jake greeted as his fingers brushed the brim of his hat. Before the women had a chance to reply, he was already gathering Lily in his arms and cradling her as if she was the most precious thing on the face of the planet. For once, the move didn't make Teddy's eyes roll. He finally understood.

"Boo!" Alice heckled. "It can't be time to go already, I've only just convinced Laney here to sing 'Single Ladies' with me."

"Neither of you are single." Jake smirked, his hands tightening around Lily as if he were scared she was about to run away or worse, join Alice on stage for a "Single Ladies" rendition.

"No shit, Sherlock," Alice replied, accompanied by an overly dramatic sigh.

Teddy ignored the jibes starting to fly between brother- and sister-in-law and turned his attention back to the stage. Just in time as his gaze collided with Summer's.

Mid-lyric she jumped and let out a squeal into the mic. He couldn't have stopped the smile spreading across his face, even if he wanted to. Nor could he stop his feet from moving toward her. Especially after realizing her intentions as the mic thudded against the floor.

Seconds later, Summer was throwing herself off the stage and into Teddy's arms.

"Teddy!" She shrieked as her fingernails dug into his

shoulder blades. "Did you like my song?"

"Yeah, doll, I liked your song." Humor laced his voice as she wriggled and writhed in his grasp. "How much have you had to drink, baby?" His hands moved to her ass as her legs wrapped around his waist.

"Uh"—she not-so-daintily hiccupped—"two?"

A laugh vibrated through him. "Two what? Bottles?"

Burying her face in Teddy's neck, Summer started to giggle. Damn. She was adorable.

Enjoying the feel of her secured safely in his hold, he started back toward the table. On the way back, her giggles dissipated, and her intentions turned torturous. Open-mouthed kisses crept up his neck until his steps faltered. "Doll," he warned in his sternest tone.

Her warm breath sent a shiver down his spine as her lips hovered over his ear. "I want you." Her voice had taken on a huskier quality, forcing Teddy to stifle a groan. "I've been thinking about you all night. How you touch me. How you taste. How you feel inside …"

Summer's whispers elicited a primal growl. A growl that undoubtedly hadn't gone unnoticed. All eyes had been on them since she'd jumped off stage and into his arms. Now he was growling like an animal as his woman's words penetrated him, making his whole body pulsate. Thank God she was wrapped around him, protecting what was left of his dignity.

"Jesus Christ, you two," Ivy chastised as Teddy finally made it to the table. "If I wasn't so close to hurling, I'd suggest that you get a room."

"Oh, please, like I haven't walked in on you and Ace re-enacting scenes you'd only find on the discovery channel." Teddy grinned, loving the shade of red his sister had now turned.

"Okay, children." Jake chuckled. "Time to go. Me and my lovely wife have plans."

After a few groans, Jake eventually managed to herd the other women toward the exit. Teddy followed closely behind, Summer still in his arms. Now to get her home. His home. In his bed. Where she belonged.

***

Teddy tugged at his collar again. Damn monkey suit. After years of uniforms, you'd think he'd be used to being uncomfortable. But three years of flannel seemed to be enough to have his body rebelling.

It's only for a few hours.

Knocking once on Ivy's bedroom door, he hadn't been prepared for the sight that greeted him as it swung open.

Wow.

"Wow, sis"—he let out a heavy breath—"shit. You look … fuck."

"You always did have a way with words, bro." Ivy shoved his shoulder, a wide smile pulling at her lips.

He needed to pull himself together. Tell his sister she looked unreal. Stunning. Beautiful. But his throat had tightened to the point of pain. It hit him then, hard. Their family was growing. For the first time. Ever. All they'd known was loss. All they'd had for so long was each other. But no more. Today their tiny family unit of two would expand. Not just to include Ace, but to include his family too.

"Hey." Ivy's smile wavered as she lay a hand on his chest. "You okay?"

He tried to cough through the tightness and ignored the mist clouding his vision. "Yeah. You look fucking amazing, sis. Goddamn stunning."

Teddy glanced down at the simple, strapless white dress that hugged her small frame and flared out when it reached her knees. Her crystal-encrusted heels had given her enough height that her face now reached his shoulders, offering him a clear view of her perfectly applied makeup. All made up she should look different. A world away from his tomboy sister who lived in mud-stained jeans and boots. But she didn't. She still managed to look like herself. She even wore her signature braid. Well, a much fancier version of it.

"Only you could curse in your compliments, Teddy." A light laugh escaped as she ran her hands self-consciously over her dress.

He tugged one of her hands off the pristine fabric and encompassed it with his own. "Seriously, Ivy. You look beautiful. Ace is gonna lose his mind." Teddy watched as she sucked in a breath. No doubt trying to reign in the same emotions he was also battling with. "It really is an honor to walk you down the aisle. I'm so proud of you."

She fell into his arms then. Teddy's hands gently encircled her, ensuring his hold wasn't too tight. He was all too aware of the fact that she needed to keep her hair, makeup, and outfit intact.

"I wish they were here," she mumbled into his suit. He didn't need her to clarify who she was talking about.

"They are, darlin', I know it. They're up there looking down on us. I can hear Mom now, screaming down at me, telling me not to let you cry and ruin your makeup. And Dad, well, he's trying to get me to hurl a few threats Ace's way. Something along the lines of … 'You hurt her, you die.'"

He heard a watery laugh as she squeezed him tight. "I love you, Teddy."

"Love you too, sis."

He kept hold of her. Silence falling between the two of them as they attempted to fight back tears.

Eventually, Ivy pulled away. Her smile firmly back in place. "Let's do this."

Holding out his arm, he waited for her to grasp onto him, and then led the way.

Once they were outside, his own grin stretched as wide as it could go. Summer really had done an amazing job of making this wedding special. Chairs stood on either side of the makeshift aisle. Each had a white covering and was completed with a blue silk bow. Blue hydrangeas lined the path toward the stage where Ace stood, still facing the officiant.

As they took their place at the edge of the white carpet runner, Ivy's hand trembled against Teddy's forearm. Placing a hand over it, he leaned down to whisper in her ear. "That man loves you more than life itself. You've got this, sis. Let's get you hitched, huh?"

Looking up at him with wide eyes, she gave him a single nod. He gave his own nod to the officiant. All at once, guests rose, music began to play, and Ace turned around.

As they walked down the aisle, Teddy's gaze was glued to his soon-to-be brother-in-law, who looked positively awestruck. The closer they got, the heavier the rise and fall of Ace's chest. And the mistier both their eyes became. Teddy may be giving his sister away, but he was leaving her in good hands.

***

"Have I told you how sexy you look in a suit?" Summer's hands slipped under his jacket and rested on his chest.

They'd danced through at least four songs, reluctant to let each other go.

"Have *I told you* how hot you look in this sexy silk dress?" Teddy countered, his hands skimming down until they met the curve of her ass.

Thanks to his amazing girlfriend, his sister's wedding had gone off without a hitch. They were now all enjoying the dinner and dancing portion of the evening. With many guests still milling by the buffet tables while others, including the bride and groom, swayed on the dancefloor.

"Wait until you see what I'm wearing under it."

He jerked and drew back just enough to get a good look at her sultry smile. "Baby." He groaned. "You trying to kill me here?"

Dragging him closer, she tugged his head forward until her lips brushed his ear. "I'm not wearing any panties."

Lord have mercy on me.

"Summer, I swear to God, you're gonna pay for that." He pulled back to see his warning had only made her smile wider. "You think you're funny, huh?"

"Oh, I *know* I'm funny."

A tickling assault followed as his fingers took advantage of their newfound knowledge of her most sensitive spots. "Really? Who's funny now, doll?"

"No!" Summer laughed, shrieked, and struggled to get away. "Stop it! No fair!" His hands continued their onslaught while he was unable to keep his own laughter at bay. "Oh my God, Teddy! Stop it! You're making a scene!"

"Guys." Ace's commanding tone gave Teddy's fingers a momentary pause. "Hate to break up the fun, but it's time for the speeches."

Summer jumped out of his reach, victory written all over her pretty little face as she pointed in his direction. "Ha!"

Ace looked between the two of them and chuckled under his breath. "You two are ridiculous. Come on, back to your seats."

They both complied, trying their hardest to keep a straight face as they playfully smacked each other's asses on the way back to their table.

As he settled into his own seat, he watched as Summer sat down before quickly jumping back up. "What's up?"

"Shit. The gift I got for Ivy ... it's back at my apartment."

"So? We'll drop it off tomorrow." He reached for her hand to steady her.

"No, they're going on their honeymoon tomorrow. I should go get it."

Was she serious? "Doll, it'll keep. Sit back down; we'll give it to her when they get back."

"No, I'm gonna go get it." Summer grabbed her keys from her purse and laid it back down on the table, "I'll be quick. Fifteen-twenty minutes tops."

"Wait"—he stood—"I'll go with you."

"Don't be silly. You're giving a speech, remember?" She stretched up to kiss his cheek. "I'll be back before you know it. I promise."

After snaring her lips and giving her a good reason to hurry back to him, he begrudgingly let her go. A funny feeling settled in his stomach as she walked away. It had to be the steak he'd eaten earlier. Right?

CHAPTER FOURTEEN

Summer parked a few doors down from Mickey's. The town was eerily quiet. Although she suspected shutting the only bar in Bluestone down for the day probably had something to do with that.

Despite enjoying a warm spring day, now the sun had set, the cool night air forced her to hug her frame as she quickened her pace.

How could she have forgotten the necklace? She'd been so excited to gift it to Ivy. It had been passed down to Summer by her grandmother. Not technically an heirloom, but it did have sentimental value. Ivy had always been like a sister to her, so it felt only right to pass it on to her. On her special day.

Maybe you should have been thinking with your brain this morning instead of your hormones?

Where was the fun in that? She felt her stomach flutter as she thought back to this morning. But before she could bask in the fever-inducing flashbacks, a tight grip on her elbow had her crying out in pain. A forceful yank and a powerful push later and she'd been backed into the alley next to Mickey's and pinned to the cold brick wall.

As her eyes began to focus again, acid rose up her throat

as she glimpsed into the familiar gray eyes of her ex. Ben.

"It's about time you showed up." He sneered.

"W-what are you doing here?" Damnit, everything was shaking. Even her words.

"What do *you* think I'm doing here, Summer? I've come to see my girlfriend. Find out why she's been avoiding me."

Was he fucking insane? "I'm not your girlfriend, Ben. I haven't been for a very long time."

"Bullshit," he spat, "I say when and *if* we break up, babe. And we're not done here. Not by a long shot."

Yes. He is fucking insane.

Both his hands were now on her, fingers brutally digging into her biceps, ensuring she wasn't going anywhere anytime soon. Her mind raced, trying desperately to think of something, anything, that might help her. Sadly, reading up on how to deal with psycho ex-boyfriends who drag you into alleys hadn't come up on her to-do list recently, and she was coming up short.

Hang on.

Teddy had made her watch *The Negotiator* the other night, surely she could remember something useful from that. Couldn't she? This was definitely a hostage type of situation.

You're never supposed to say no *when negotiating. That's what Samuel L. Jackson said anyway. Shit. Is that all I took from a two-fricking-hour movie?*

Okay. So, she wasn't supposed to say no. She also probably shouldn't be in a dark alley with him either. There was a sort of plan there. Somewhere. Step one, try not to say no. Step two, get out of the alley. Simple.

"Maybe we could talk about this over coffee? There's a diner just around the corner from here. Why don't we head on over there?" No one said she had to be subtle.

He let out a humorless laugh that sent chills through her. "I'm not fucking stupid, Summer. The moment you get a chance … you'll try and run again. Maybe call that new man of yours."

How the hell did he know about Teddy? Then it dawned

on her. He'd been watching her. Waiting for his chance to pounce. To get her alone.

"That's right. I know about *him*. What a whore you've been."

The venom lacing his words managed to flip some kind of switch inside her. She finally seemed to realize the seriousness of the situation. This was bad. Really bad. This man had hit her before. Repeatedly. And he'd sounded just like this when he'd done it. Now here she was, alone with him. In a stupid alley. In a deserted town because everyone was back at Moonrock celebrating Ivy and Ace's marriage.

Fuck. Fuck. Fuck.

Fight or flight kicked in as he began to shake her, slamming her back into the brick wall over and over again. She knew this pattern. She'd been here before. He'd use his fists next. Maybe drag her around by the hair.

Ben's momentary surprise at her struggle worked in her favor. His grip loosened on one arm, and she managed to free it from his grasp. It allowed her to deliver a hard shove to his chest, propelling him backward and saving her back from another sharp blow.

Unfortunately, he recovered quickly. Too quickly. Her free arm did not stay free for long.

"You fucking bitch." He twisted one arm and used it to spin her around until his chest was pressing into her back. "You'll pay for that."

She tried to relax her body and slump against him. She remembered someone saying that it was easier to get out of a hold if your body was loose. Now, what was she supposed to do next? Was it drop or kick? Damnit. Self-defense classes would be first on her list if she got out of this.

She chose to kick. A hard strike against his shin. He definitely wasn't expecting that. Although he kept hold of her, she was able to thrash enough to make him stumble. Just as she thought she was making progress though, his hand shot out. A hard punch to the back had her falling to the floor. Which wouldn't have been so bad had her hands been able to break her fall. But they were still behind her. Only being released by Ben at the last second. A second too late.

Her head met the concrete just as an angry sounding "hey" was shouted down the alley. A voice she recognized. Colt. Another fricking ex. What was it, bring-your-ex-to-an-alley day? And then it went black.

CHAPTER FIFTEEN

Teddy looked at his watch again. Where on earth was Summer? Twenty minutes his ass. She'd been gone almost an hour now. After forty minutes he'd tried to call her, only to realize she'd left her phone there. In her purse. Then he'd tried calling her landline. Then the bar. But nothing. No answer. Seeing as she'd taken his truck, he was currently considering some sort of smoke signal.

"You look like you're about to give the buffet table a beatdown, man, you okay?" Jake collapsed into the seat next to him.

"Yeah. No. I don't know." Teddy scrubbed his face in frustration.

"Well, that clears that up." Jake continued to eye him cautiously.

Teddy's gaze went back to the house. His eyes had been straying there for the past hour, hoping to get a glimpse of Summer swaying back over to him. Maybe then the roiling in his gut would stop.

"Sorry, man, it's just Summer's supposed to be back by now … she took my truck to go pick something up from the apartment and then she was gonna come straight back." He flicked his eyes back to Jake. "I'm worried. I can't get a hold of her."

Understanding, Jake nodded before reaching into his back pocket. "Here, take my truck." Teddy caught the keys tossed at him. "Go check on her."

"You sure?"

"Yeah, man. Go check on your woman. Hell, you don't even need to bring it back—party's almost over anyways. Keep it and I'll pick it up tomorrow. Lily and I will hitch a lift with Ali and Brady."

Teddy was out of his seat before Jake had even finished talking. Grabbing Summer's purse, he offered his friend a chin lift and was on the move.

Thankful he'd only indulged in one drink; he climbed into Jake's truck and started the engine. His mind was still all over the place and his stomach continued to flip. Something was wrong. He could feel it.

The longest ten minutes of his life ensued as he envisioned everything from a car accident to Summer falling down the stairs and breaking her ankle.

As he finally drove down main street, it didn't take him long to spot his truck. That had to be a good sign. Surely. It meant Summer was still at the apartment. Then why didn't he feel better?

"Keep it together, man," he mumbled as he parked and jumped out. Headed straight to the bar, it took no time at all to reach Mickey's.

The bar was locked, dark, and empty. After switching on the lights, he rounded the bar and headed for the back stairwell leading up to Summer's apartment. Even though he was mildly relieved not to find her injured at the bottom of the staircase, he was all too aware of how quiet it was. And dark. If she'd have been there, she hadn't switched on any lights.

Taking the stairs two at a time, he unlocked the door only to find more darkness. Cursing under his breath, he flicked them on and did a quick check of the apartment. Empty.

Damnit. Where is she?

Now he was starting to panic. This wasn't some bad movie. People didn't just disappear. Something bad had to have happened. He knew it. Every hair on the back of his neck pricked up. Every muscle tightened. His heart began thumping for freedom.

Minutes later, he was outside Mickey's, phone in hand. He stared intently at the glowing screen as if it had all the answers. No calls. No messages. And still no freaking clue. Trying to decide who to call first, the police or the hospital, he began to pace the street. His foot froze mid-step as he got to the side alley. A splash of blood on the concrete caught his attention.

No. No. No.

As he crouched above the red stain, his body began to shake.

Please don't let that be her blood. Please let her be okay.

Scrambling to dial the hospital, he didn't take a single breath until he'd hung up. And even then, he wasn't sure how he was still managing to get enough air into his lungs. The sympathetic receptionist's words, "unconscious," "brain injury," and "ICU" flashing through his mind at a million miles an hour.

I never told her that I loved her.

The drive to the hospital happened in a daze. To keep him focused, he called Brady. First and foremost, he wanted the local deputy to call the sheriff and find out what the hell happened. Secondly, he entrusted the man to let everyone know what happened and where he would be.

Storming reception like a bat out of hell, the teenage-looking receptionist shrank into her seat as he approached the desk.

"Summer Willis." He grunted. "I was told she's in ICU. I want to see her ... talk to her doctor. Get an update."

"Uh, are you family?"

"I'm her fiancé," he ground out through clenched teeth. It wasn't technically a lie. He planned to be just that very soon if he had his way.

If she gets through this.

"Okay, sir, if you want to make your way up to the second floor and take a seat, I'll let the attending physician know you're here."

Teddy thanked her and made his way upstairs. Plastic seats weren't going to cut it right now though. But he couldn't exactly pace around the waiting room like a caged animal either. Instead, he found a spot to wring his hands against the wall. Next to a coffee machine.

He checked his phone again. Still no word from Brady.

Why the fuck didn't I tell her I loved her? What if I never get another chance? Oh God, please let her be okay.

He let his head fall into his hands. He was a goddamn Navy SEAL and he'd never felt so helpless in his whole damn life.

"Willis family?"

Teddy's head lifted, his gaze finding a graying, pudgy man in a white coat. "Yeah," he croaked as he made his way toward the doctor. "Teddy McCallen, Summer's fiancé."

The older man took his outstretched hand and shook it. "Teddy, I'm Dr. Burke. If you'd like to follow me, I'll take you to see Ms. Willis. I can then give you an update on her condition."

"Is she awake?" He couldn't stop hope from blooming.

"No." Dr. Burke started toward the corridor; Teddy followed behind. "She's stable but hasn't regained consciousness yet."

Hasn't regained consciousness. I don't need to be a doctor to know that's not good.

"Do you know what happened?"

"According to the man who brought her in, she fell headfirst onto the ground. Concrete I believe."

Wait. What? "The man who brought her in? Is he still here? Do you know who he was?"

Teddy followed the doctor into the sterile white room. The smell of antiseptic immediately seeping into his skin.

Even knowing what he did, he felt utterly unprepared for the sight of Summer. Hooked up to a series of tubes, wires and cables, steady beeps interrupting the sudden ringing in his ears.

"I'm afraid I don't have a name or any more information. Now." Dr. Burke gestured at the bed. "According to her CT scan, the fall caused some minor swelling on Ms. Willis's brain. As she is yet to wake up, we want to monitor her blood and oxygen levels overnight." Okay. The ringing in Teddy's ears was back. "We're hoping that it will go down naturally over the next few days and there won't be a need for surgery."

Surgery. Jesus. "Brain surgery?" Even the words made him gulp.

"Yes. To relieve the pressure. But for now, we want to wait. See if the swelling goes down on its own."

Teddy slumped into the chair next to Summer's bed. Reaching for her hand, he was careful of the wires as he placed his big hand over her small one.

"Now, technically visiting hours are over. But … in this case, I think we can make an exception."

Teddy nodded at the doctor in thanks before retraining his eyes on the fragile form before him.

"I'll be back later to check on her."

Teddy didn't look up again but heard the door close behind him. She looked so frail. So breakable. How could things go from so good to so, so bad in the span of only a few hours? And why the hell did he still not have any answers as to how they got this way?

Scooting his chair closer to her bed, he scraped along the vinyl until he couldn't go any further. This is where he needed to be. Beside her. Holding her hand. Until she wakes up and he sees those beautiful hazel eyes, he wasn't going anywhere.

"I love you, baby; I love you so fucking much. Come back to me, okay? We're gonna get through this."

***

Teddy jolted awake to find Brady standing at the end of Summer's hospital bed, frowning.

"Hey," Teddy wheezed as he sat straighter in his chair, "what time is it?"

"Seven." Brady cleared his throat. "Sorry, I couldn't get here earlier, I was down at the station."

That woke Teddy up. "You find out what happened? How my woman ended up in a damn hospital bed?"

He watched as his friend's hand ran through his messy dark hair. He looked just as rough as Teddy felt. Clearly Brady hadn't slept. He hadn't even changed, still wearing a now-creased suit.

"Yeah, man, I did." He sighed and shot Summer another look before turning his attention to Teddy. "We have her ex in custody, a Ben Davis. According to our witness statement, he was caught struggling with her in the alley next to Mickey's."

Teddy's chair screeched back as he pushed up, rising to his full height. He gritted his teeth. Adrenaline spiking his blood. "Her motherfucking ex did this to her? He's here in Bluestone?"

"Easy, man," Brady warned, "he's in custody. Which means as much as you want to … you can't beat the shit out of him. Let us handle it, okay? He's not getting away with this. I promise you that."

Teddy's chest heaved. Anger coursing through his veins, and the pulse in his neck threatening to explode. He was going to kill Ben fucking Davis. Rip him limb from limb. How dare he lay a hand on Summer? How dare he scare her? Hurt her? He would make him pay. Somehow. Someway.

"He hurt her, Brady. She's fucking unconscious. Goddamn swelling on her brain! I swear to God, unless you lock him up and throw away the key, he's a fucking dead man."

"I'm gonna pretend I didn't hear that last bit, Teddy." Brady placed his hands on his hips, looking every bit a cop. "Look, we got a witness. We'll get Summer's statement *when* she wakes up. And the dude has priors. Which means he'll get jail time."

Falling back in his seat, Teddy simply grunted and took hold of Summer's hand again. Just as Brady went to leave, he realized there was one more thing he still hadn't asked. "Who's the witness?"

"Colton Brown. He got there just in time. Saw Summer hit the ground. Ben tried to run, of course, but Colt got him. Even roughed him up a little by the looks of it. Called the police and an ambulance. He did good."

Well shit. Looks like he'd have to remove Colton Brown from his hit list.

***

It had been two days and Summer still hadn't woken up. In forty-eight hours, Teddy had gone through every emotion under the sun. Scans had shown the swelling had, in fact, gone down with the help of whatever the hell was in her drips. That was the good news. The bad news was she still wasn't awake. And despite doctors and nurses reassuring him, he didn't miss the concerned glances aimed Summer's way when they came by to check on her.

"You stink." Ivy sat back down in her chair on the other side of Summer's bed.

To be honest, it was a fair assessment. Other than to go to the bathroom, he hadn't left his woman's bedside in two days. Jake, Lily, Brady, Ali, Ace, Ivy, and Laney would come and go, bringing with them food and drinks while they nagged him to go home to shower and sleep.

"Don't start." Teddy sighed, scrubbing his hand across his overgrown stubble.

"I'm just saying … if you're trying to wake her using the power of smell, then you might want to add some deodorant to the mix."

"Funny."

"Seriously, though, Teddy, you need to get some rest. Some sleep in an actual bed. You know I'll call you if anything changes."

It was that time of the visit already. "Ivy ... I'm not having this conversation again. Until she's awake, until I know she's okay, I'm not going anywhere. The idea of her waking up and me not being here ... it makes me feel sick. And don't even pretend you wouldn't do the same thing if it was Ace lying here."

Ivy went quiet. Finally. He thought that might do it. There was no way in hell his sister would leave her husband alone for one second if the situation was reversed.

"I get it," Ivy whispered.

"I don't know that you do. I shoulda told her, Ivy." His throat felt raw. "I shoulda told her every second of every day how I felt. How much I love her. That she's the only one for me. I spent my whole life wanting her, wanting to tell her just how gone for her I am, and what do I do when I finally get her? I choke. That's right, when shit gets real, I choke. And now she's lying in that bed, fighting for her life, not knowing how loved she is."

Ivy was up and out of her seat before he'd finished his last sentence. She crouched in front of him and dragged him into a hug he never knew he needed until now. It had been a long two days. Every time he closed his eyes he was back in Iraq, only instead of seeing Mason's lifeless body, he saw Summer's. Needless to say, he hadn't slept much.

Teddy soaked up his sister's comfort. Thankful that his punishing internal monologue had quietened down. At least for the time being. They stayed like that for a while. Enough for his heartbeat to steady.

All that calm lasted a total of two minutes, as the sound of Summer gasping beside him had his heart missing more than a few beats.

CHAPTER SIXTEEN

Holy shit, my head hurts.

Summer couldn't get her eyes to open any wider. It wasn't quite a squint she was sporting, more like a rapid succession of blinks.

"Ivy, hit the lights."

She recognized that voice. Teddy. Of course Teddy was there. Her knight in shining armor. Witness to yet another mistake that managed to bleed over into his life now too.

Wait. Did he say Ivy? Shouldn't she be on her honeymoon?

No. Please no.

"Doll." His voice was closer now. She tried again to open her eyes. It was easier this time. Darker. "That's it. Open those beautiful eyes for me."

"Hey." It was nice to know she sounded just as awful as she felt.

Trying to move her face to look around, she winced at the shooting pains striking her right in the head. Oh dear. Everything hurt. Even her hair hurt.

"Hey, baby." Teddy's meaty fingers lightly ran over her cheeks. "How you doing? How are your pain levels?"

Is fifty fucking million a level?

Before she had a chance to answer, the room was flooded. Ivy was followed in by two nurses and someone Summer could only assume was a doctor. The stethoscope gave him away. Teddy was pushed aside as the women fussed over the machines and the lines currently attached to her.

Once she'd been thoroughly examined, the questions began. More pain-level guessing. Sadly, fifty fucking million was not recognized as an official measurement of pain-level assessment.

She felt Teddy's hot gaze on her throughout. The longer his stare penetrated her, the more anxious she felt. It was one thing to see her looking like this, it was another for him to witness the result of her stupidity. What must he think of her? It wasn't cute to be this much of a hot mess so far into your thirties.

Just when she thought she couldn't possibly feel any worse, the doctor explained exactly what had happened. What her body had been through. And what to expect over the next few days. Goddamn brain swelling. Her brain had actually swelled. She hadn't even known that was a thing. Scared, overwhelmed, mad as hell. Those sentiments were just the tip of the iceberg when it came to the emotions bubbling up to the surface.

That motherfucker.

"Did you catch him … Ben?" That question was directed at Teddy as the room began to clear.

"Yeah, doll, you're safe. He was taken into custody."

"Before … I remember hearing Colt. Is he okay?"

She watched as Teddy settled into the chair next to her bed and captured her hand. Lacing his fingers through hers.

"He's good. He's actually the one who called the ambulance and got you here. He also restrained Ben until the cops arrived."

"He did?" Wow. Maybe he wasn't the devil after all.

"Yeah, doll, he did. I think I'm gonna have to un-bar him from Mickey's."

She tried to smile, but it hurt. It was probably a good thing she didn't allow the mood to lighten though. What she was about to ask Teddy likely wouldn't go down well.

"Teddy?" She cringed at her scratchy voice.

"Yeah, baby?"

"I need you to do something for me."

"Anything, baby, anything you need." He squeezed her hand reassuringly.

Here goes nothing.

"I need some time … to process everything. Some space. What Ben did …" She shivered as her mind unhelpfully replayed that night. "Honestly? I'm a mess, Teddy. What he did. What I felt … am still feeling … What I'm trying to say is that I'm gonna be a mess for a while and it's not fair—"

"Whoa," he cut her off, "if you're about to say it's not fair on me … you can stop right now. 'Cause that is some bullshit. I want to be there for you. I want to help you through this. Please let me. Please, baby?"

You can do this. It's the right thing to do.

Summer's eyes closed. Not from the pain in her head this time but from the new ache in her chest.

"You said you'd do anything. This is what I need. This is what I want. My head is all fucked up … *literally*. You heard the doctor. Please. If you care about me at all, you'll do this for me. Please, Teddy." She wasn't beyond begging at this point. Anything to make this feeling inside of her go away.

Teddy was quiet for a moment before he surprised her by asking, "How long?"

"I don't know."

A weird noise emanated from his chest. A cross between a growl and a groan. Whatever it was, it didn't sound good. "You're still in hospital, still recovering … I only just got you back, and now you're asking me to walk away? For God knows how long? What the hell, Summer? That's not fair."

She opened her eyes and immediately regretted it when she got a look at his. Green flashes of hurt awaited her, causing a sting. "I know it's not fair. I know I should be grateful you're even here after what I put you through. I know I don't deserve you. But ... I need this. I need time to process. On my own. Recover mentally as well as physically. I can't do that when I'm feeling guilty for dragging you into my drama. This is all my fault. Another bad decision has come back to haunt me, and I can't stand the thought that you're now paying the price too. That's the last thing you need or deserve, Teddy."

"Jesus Christ, Summer." Teddy roughly ran his hand over his head. "Grateful? Fucking guilty? You're breaking my heart here, doll. You're wrong. This isn't your fault. *Nothing* about this is your fault. Don't you *ever* let that motherfucker make you feel like it was or that you're less than. And as for me—"

"Teddy—"

"I'm not finished. I'll give you your space, dollface. But this is *not* the fucking end ... You hear me? I'll wait as long as it takes. As long as you need. And when you're ready, I'm gonna spend my life showing you just *how* deserving you are."

And with that, Teddy stalked out of the room. She got what she wanted. Hadn't she? Then why did it feel so wrong?

***

The next few days were hard. Despite a never-ending stream of visitors, Summer had never felt more alone. It was becoming abundantly clear that she'd sent away the only person she wanted to see.

Every day had become a battle between her heart and her head. And it didn't help that Teddy was playing dirty.

Shortly after he'd left, Lily dropped off a bag full of things she'd need for the remainder of her stay at the hospital. Packed by Teddy. It contained everything she would have picked out for herself given the chance. From her favorite pajamas, down to the exact number of cotton pads she used to tone her face every night. She wanted to be annoyed at how predictable she was, instead, it only made her ache. Why did he have to know her so well?

He'd also used their friends to sneak in thoughtful contraband for her on a daily basis. The first day it was a box containing three various slices of pie with a note reading, *Only forty-four more flavors to go.* The second day it was a bottle of her preferred sweet tea. And today, Laney had snuck in her favorite trashy magazines, along with a giant pallet of strawberries. It was official. She was the biggest bitch on the planet.

"So … are we gonna talk about the proverbial elephant in the room, or continue to pretend everything is fine?" Laney eyed her as Summer bit into another strawberry.

"Um, hello?" Summer gestured over her cotton pajamas. "I'm in a hospital bed after my ex-boyfriend attacked me in an alley, I think we can safely say that everything is *not* fine."

"Cute. You know exactly what I'm talking about, Summer. *Who* I'm talking about. One six-foot-four, grumpy, pain in my ass who has practically been stalking me since you kicked him to the curb."

"Stalking you?"

"Yes, honey. Stalking me. He calls me day and night to check on you, not to mention all the frigging text messages. *How's she doing today? Has her color returned? Did she manage to keep any food down?* The man has it baaaaad."

Butterflies began to swarm Summer's stomach. He hadn't given up on her. She knew he said that he wouldn't, but doing and saying were completely different things.

"He deserves so much better than me, Lanes."

"What are you even talking about?"

"Come on, Laney. Be real. I take baggage to a whole new level. I'm like the epitome of damaged goods. Crazy exes. Mommy and daddy issues. An anxiety disorder. Oh, and let's not forget that if it wasn't for Teddy, I'd be jobless *and* homeless right now."

Her best friend shook her head. Looking almost disappointed. "Well damn. I guess I should start shopping for a new friend, huh? One who isn't such a disaster."

Summer shot her a look that hopefully conveyed how not funny she was being. Sarcasm really didn't suit her. "You really suck at this friend thing. Maybe *I'm* the one who should be shopping around. Aren't you supposed to tell me that I'm wrong? Try and make me feel better?"

Laney simply laughed and stole another strawberry. "Huh, let me see. First off, you do have crazy exes … well, one at least. Your mommy and daddy issues stem from them being total and utter assholes—I'm not sure you can do much about that. De-asshole-ification isn't a thing yet. And then there's your anxiety. I get that it's a bitch … but it's also not as uncommon as you might think. Plus, it can be easy to control once you get to the root of it."

"De-asshole-ification?" Summer couldn't fight the smile tipping up her lips. "Do you have a point?"

"Of course I do." Laney paused to chew the strawberry she'd been nibbling on throughout her little speech. "My point is, yes, you have shit going on. But who the hell doesn't? Or even cares? Teddy certainly doesn't. Plus, it's not like you have any more baggage than the next person. If anything, Teddy is the one with baggage in this relationship. Not you."

"No. He doesn't. He's fricking perfect and you know it."

"Oh, really? So, you don't think he has just as many insecurities as you? A retired Navy SEAL orphan?"

God, Summer really hated Laney sometimes. And she told her just that. "I hate you."

"No, you don't. You love me." She winked and went back to stealing her strawberries.

***

Two days later, Summer got the all-clear and was currently being discharged. After Laney had given her a stern talking to, she'd been more than motivated to get her act together.

She'd started by giving her statement to Brady and agreeing to press charges. Ben needed to pay. One way or another. She would not live in fear any longer. Lucky for her, he was still being held. Turns out good old Ben had a record. One he'd managed to hide from the aid agency and one that was now preventing him from making bail.

Her mommy and daddy issues were trickier. They weren't exactly going to be solved overnight, but in the name of extending an olive branch she had given them a call. She'd even told them about what had happened with Ben. They'd been surprisingly sympathetic. Not so much that they were on the first flight to Montana, but enough that they suggested a visit in the near future. That would have to do for now.

She'd also spoken to her doctor about her anxiety. She was in a hospital after all, she might as well make use of all the experts milling around. Dr. Burke had recommended talking to someone as a first step and had helped her get a referral. It was only a matter of time now before she became the poster child for good mental health.

Then, of course, there was Teddy. He never strayed too far from her thoughts. And she'd finally come to a decision. One that was best for both of them.

"Ready?" Laney chirped as she grabbed Summer's bag.

"As I'll ever be."

CHAPTER SEVENTEEN

Dear Lord, give me patience.

A prayer Teddy knew would go unanswered. The last of his patience had gone out of the window, the same time Kelly had dropped her third tray of the night. Nothing was going right tonight. In fact, nothing had been going right since he'd been dismissed from Summer's side five long days ago.

If it hadn't been for Laney's updates, he wouldn't have been able to hold himself back from storming the hospital and demanding she tell him exactly how she was feeling. God, he missed her.

"Good news. Jacob can come in and help; he's on his way now," Kelly beamed as she re-emerged from the back and resumed serving.

"Thank God." Teddy plonked down Bob's pint and took the old man's money. "Place is packed—it's like the whole of Bluestone decided to come out tonight."

"Isn't that a good thing?" Kelly smirked as she squirted soda over ice.

Teddy simply grunted. It was becoming increasingly difficult to disguise his bad mood from both his customers and his staff.

As he poured yet another beer, his thoughts drifted back to Summer. Who was he kidding? They'd never stopped being about Summer. What she was doing. How she was feeling. If she was thinking about him. He was a man obsessed. He'd even started to wonder what exactly constituted stalking.

Don't be that guy, man. Not cool.

Thanks to his Summer-riddled brain, the sight of her walking into Mickey's didn't register until she was standing directly in front of him. Well, in front of the bar he was behind anyway. He had to blink a few too many times. He was even considering pinching himself but thought twice about it.

She looked beautiful. Fresh-faced with her messy blonde hair sweeping all over the place. She was in jeans, a gray tank top, and her Converse. As his eyes swept over her and drank the sight of her in, it didn't take a genius to work out she was nervous. Teeth were digging into her lower lip as she fiddled with the collection of black bracelets adorning her wrist.

"Summer—"

"Please," she immediately cut him off. "Can I go first?"

Holding his breath, he reluctantly nodded and ignored the quietening crowd surrounding them.

"So, uh, this might have been a bit easier if I'd have gone with my first instinct and walked in here with a boombox over my head, playing Green Day. But when I googled *grand romantic gestures* … the internet advised that *me* doing one wasn't a good idea. Apparently women shouldn't do the whole romantic gestures thing because … and I quote … it makes them look 'too thirsty.' I'm not sure what that means … but going by all the *Fatal Attraction*-themed comments I read, I'm thinking it's not a good thing."

His smile was stretched so wide it should be hurting. But nothing. Not one goddamn thing was going to wipe this smile off his face. Summer had googled grand romantic gestures. For him. For his sorry ass.

"I guess this could be considered one anyway though, seeing as the whole bar is kinda staring at us." She wasn't wrong. "But I want it on record that I'm not doing this because I'm ..." He watched her air quote the word "thirsty."

"Noted." Humor laced his voice. Not because this was funny, but because he was so happy.

"Okay. Um. So, while you were proving just how well you knew me these past few days, I got to thinking about all the things I know about you. More specifically, all the things I love about you." *Did she just say love?* "So here goes ..."

He watched, his heart violently pounding as Summer removed a crumpled piece of paper from her jean pocket and unfolded it. She'd written a list. Jesus Christ.

"Your smile," she began. "Not only does it light up the whole room, but it somehow has the ability to actually warm me from the inside out."

It wasn't just his heart pounding now; his ears had got in on the action.

"How much you care," she continued. "For your sister, for me, for the whole town. You think I don't see you helping Dotty with her deliveries? Or helping Bob open the gift shop shutters every morning? We *all* see you."

His mouth was so dry he was finding it hard to swallow.

"How safe you make me feel. And not just since I've been back. You've always made me feel safe. And so damn strong. It's like I know ... I know that as long as I have you by my side, everything will always be okay." Her eyes finally lifted from the paper and met his. "But mostly, Teddy ... I love that you're my best friend."

He couldn't breathe. He knew he had to say something, but words were failing him. Everything was failing him. He simply wasn't functioning.

"I love you, Teddy McCallen. It's always been you." And with those words, he finally woke up. He was jumping over the bar a second later. "I'm sorry I sent you away, I didn't mean—"

She didn't get to finish her unnecessary apology because his mouth was on hers before anything else could come out. She tasted like sweet tea. Heaven.

When they eventually came up for air, she mumbled, "Do you forgive me?" against his lips.

He drew his head back just enough to catch the shine in her eyes. "Doll, there is nothing to forgive. Although truth be told, I am a little pissed that you got to be the one to say I love you first."

"You love me?" The beginnings of a smile tipped up one side of her mouth.

"Baby ... I love you so fucking much it hurts." He dropped his forehead against hers, needing to touch her again. "Don't ever send me away again, okay? I can't live without you, doll. I need you. The past few days have been torture."

"I promise," she whispered.

He needed another taste. Capturing her lips again, he breathed her in. Vanilla filling his lungs and his heart beating so loudly it drowned out the cheers and catcalls filling the bar.

Very aware of their audience, he was careful to keep his hands to himself, only letting them drift as far as her lower back. But the urge to drag her soft curves up against him was strong. Especially when she pushed her tongue deeper, making him want to beat his chest.

They continued to kiss way longer than was probably acceptable, considering where they were. It was definitely long enough to turn his blood molten. He knew they needed to stop before he took her right there on the bar floor. But he didn't. As if sensing his lack of control, Summer was the one to draw back.

They were both panting when she did. Their eyes glazed. Still standing close enough to swallow each other's breaths.

"So, I figured something out when I was in the hospital." Summer's chest heaved, brushing against him as she spoke.

"Oh yeah?" Teddy was back to smiling.

"Yeah. I'm actually not bad at relationships after all. I was just trying to do them with the wrong people. The reason it never worked out was because … they weren't you. No one was ever you."

He let himself groan. "Keep saying shit like that to me, doll, and I'm gonna drag you upstairs and have my wicked way with you."

"Oh really?"

He watched her playfully cock her eyebrow.

"Really."

"Does that mean you don't want to know that you were all I've thought about this week? How every second I wasn't with you, I was thinking about you. Wishing you were with me. Holding me. Kissing—"

There was only so much a man could take. Summer was now off her feet and cradled against his chest. Giggling. Both of them ignoring the very questionable jeers as he walked them to the back stairwell.

Summer was back to torturing him as her mouth latched onto his neck. But it was okay. Of all the possible problems to have, this was a good one.

EPILOGUE

Three months later

"Good lord, it's the crepe paper apocalypse." Alice chuckled as she entered the high school gym.

She was fricking lucky she was carrying a box full of donations, otherwise Summer might've felt the need to defend her crepe paper paradise more sternly.

"But a very pretty apocalypse." Summer grinned, gesturing Alice over to the table placed slap bang in the middle of all the chaos.

Bluestone High's prom was just one night away, and even Summer was impressed with herself for the job she'd done planning the event. It turned out she had a knack for the whole party-planning thing. Who knew? After Ivy's wedding, she'd started receiving requests from more and more people to help plan their special events too. So now, here she was, Bluestone's one and only party planner.

"Yes, Summer. The prettiest of all apocalypses. Now … where do you want these?"

Summer made space on the table for the box and wasted no time rifling through the treasure as soon as it hit the wood. "Tell me again why you have all of this? I mean … is

155

there another use for a mustache on a stick that I don't know about?"

"Well, that one I got for Brady. See, I was trying to convince him to grow a mustache and I might or might not have followed him around wearing it for a week. You know, so he could get an idea of how distinguished he'd look with one."

Summer looked up to find her friend beaming as she held the mustache above her mouth. The woman really was something else. They both burst into giggles at the same time.

"God, you're lucky that man loves you, Ali. If you were my wife, I probably would've shoved that stick where the sun don't shine."

"You fucking love me, you liar. Plus, if I didn't have such great ideas all the time, you wouldn't have a loada cool shit like this for your photo booth."

"That is true, Ali." Summer picked up the giant mouth she'd just found and dangled it in front of them. "I mean, who else buys purple-painted lips in bulk?"

"Exactly, bitch." Alice smirked, looking awfully pleased with herself.

The rest of the afternoon was much more fun than Summer expected it to be. Instead of just dropping off her donations, Alice stayed a while to help out. Clearly not a fan of crepe paper, she helped Summer set up the tables and chairs instead. By the time her friend had left, they'd all been set up. Now all Summer had to do was decorate the tables.

Deciding whether or not to call it a day, she took a seat at one of the tables and pulled out her phone. There was no reason she couldn't check her messages while she was deciding. How was it possible that Teddy's name on her screen still had the ability to make her knees weak? Oh well. That was a question for another day. Today she would just bask. Happily, and with a wide smile on her face, she clicked on his name.

Teddy: *When you're done over there, can you come meet me in* *our spot?*

Summer checked the time the message was sent before she replied. *Huh.* An hour ago.

Summer: *Sorry, baby, just seen this. Still want me to come?*

Her phone chimed almost immediately.

Teddy: *Yes.*

Summer: *Ok, leaving now! xx*

Twenty minutes later, Summer parked up. She had no idea why she was so nervous. This was Teddy. Her Teddy. Then why was her stomach freaking the fuck out?

Calm down and get it together.

Once she'd locked up her car, she started the trek toward the hilltop. Things had been good between Teddy and her. More than good. She'd even go as far as saying things were fan-frigging-tastic.

After declaring her love for him in the middle of Mickey's, they lasted a whole week of pretending to live in separate places before they bit the bullet and decided to officially move in together. They were living in Teddy's apartment until the cabin was ready. Their dream cabin.

As she neared their spot, those darn butterflies were back. Her stomach was such a pessimist. There really was no reason for her to be feeling anxious. How many times had Teddy asked her to meet him at their spot anyway, it had to be dozens.

Yeah, when you were teenagers.

So what if this was the first time he'd asked since they'd been a couple? It didn't mean anything.

Keep telling yourself that.

That's when she heard it. Green Day. The music propelled her into motion. And then everything happened so fast. Seconds later, Teddy was in view and her heart was in her throat.

Oh. My. God.

He was on his knee. And what the hell was he holding?

Her legs shook more with every step, but she wanted to get to him. Needed to. When she came to a stop, she realized that she really needed to breathe. Why was it so frigging hard to breathe?

"Dollface." Teddy's husky voice melted into her skin, making it even harder to breathe. "You good?"

She wasn't, but she nodded anyway. And swallowed hard.

"Summer … I can't remember not loving you." She could already feel her eyes start to mist. "I was stupid enough to let you go once. I'm not gonna let that happen again. Not now that I know what it's like to be loved by you."

Okay, now she was crying. Full-blown sobbing. This had to be a new record.

"You make me so damn happy, baby. I've been walking around town with this goofy-ass smile on my face for three months and I don't see it going away ever."

Teddy opened the velvet box he'd been clinging on to for dear life to reveal a single princess cut diamond on a white gold band. It was perfect.

Holy shit.

"Marry me, Summer. Grow old with me. Let me spend the rest of my life making you as happy as you make me."

Tears hit her mouth and stung her tastebuds as her lips parted. "Yes," she whispered, instantly realizing her reply was a little too quiet. "Yes," she repeated louder. "Yes, I'll marry you."

Shaky, big fingers slid the ring onto her finger. As she peered down to take in the sight of it, she was pulled down and into Teddy, who collapsed backward and quickly adjusted her onto his lap. She didn't know which one of their hearts was beating the fastest, but they both clung to each other through their pants, as if their life depended on it.

"You've just made me the luckiest man on the planet. I love you so fucking much, baby." Teddy's voice was so deep and thick with emotion, it managed to inspire a cascade of goosebumps to prickle up over every exposed part of her body.

"I love you too, Teddy." Placing her lips over his, she breathed him in. *Mmm. Musky, manly goodness.* "So much, baby."

Impatient to taste each other, Teddy was the one to give in first and take her lips, parting them with such ease as he gripped the side of her face and held her to him. He took and took and overwhelmed her senses. His tongue claiming her deep, while his teeth scraped, and his mouth sucked until her brain was turned to mush.

She surrendered to him willingly. She was his and he was hers. Her man. Her love. Her soulmate. Forever.

SEE WHERE THE BLUESTONE SERIES BEGAN:

LOVE TOOLS

What happens when the king of casual meets the queen of picking the wrong men?

Lily is running. From a dead-end job, a neurotic mother and all the losers she dared to date. Moving halfway across the world to Bluestone County seemed like a good idea at the time. So did reopening her estranged father's hardware store. But now she isn't so sure.

Small town living has its perks though. Wide-open space, clean air, and sexy cowboys. Well, one sexy cowboy. Jake. Who also just so happens to be the new bane of her existence. At least when he's not talking, she can admire the view.

Jake is the king of casual. The love of his life has always been his ranch, and that was fine with him. He never really saw the point in long-term. But all that changes when a mouthy, blonde sasses him into oblivion. He should have known she'd be trouble as soon as he laid eyes on her. Now it's too late. She's all he can think about. All he has to do is convince her that he's finally the right man.

Isobel Reed's hilarious, emotionally charged romance will have you holding your side with laughter or reaching for a tissue. Reminiscent of small-town romance by Tessa Bailey or Kristen Ashley, you will fall in love with LOVE TOOLS and Isobel Reed's unique writing style.

EXCERPT

Lily took the opportunity to scan his face and let her eyes wander down him. His broad shoulders filled out his check shirt that pulled tight across his muscled chest. She tried her hardest not to gawk as her gaze travelled down farther to his mud-stained denim jeans that moulded perfectly to tensed thighs.

Holy shit, he's hot. Do all the men in Montana look like this?

"You about done checking me out, darlin', or do you want me to turn around and show you the back?"

She felt her cheeks flame as her eyes flicked back up and she caught sight of his cocky grin. Before she could attempt to deny what she'd been doing, his expression turned more serious as he gave her a once-over. "I didn't know Matt had a daughter."

Surprise, surprise.

"No shit. He wasn't exactly father of the year."

Lily couldn't help but think of the irony. Her father had become friends with some guy young enough to be his son, yet he still couldn't quite be bothered to pick up the phone and call his own daughter.

Marlboro Man's smile became crooked as his glare intensified. "You always swear like a trucker, darlin'? Here I thought English women were all class and manners."

Is he being fucking serious?

She let out a huff; she couldn't believe the nerve of this guy. "I'm sorry, have I stepped into the past? Are you gonna ask me why a little woman like me isn't married next?"

"All right, sweetheart, calm down." He sniggered, clearly

amused by the steam coming out of her ears.

EXPIRY DATING

Sparks start more than a fire... They start an explosion.

Alice is not happy. Her ex screwed her over, literally. One day her mother is dreaming of a white wedding, the next, Alice is hurling hardbacks at a naked boyfriend caught in bed with her best friend. So she did the only logical thing she could think of. She got the hell out of there. In fact, she left the country.

It's not long before she discovers the perks of small-town living, and she even finds herself a job. There is just one thing stopping this all from being perfect though. One infuriating person she just can't seem to shake. Brady Mitchell. It figures that the hottest man she's ever seen also just so happens to be the most annoying one on the planet.

Brady is back home and trying to come to terms with life outside the military. Adjusting to a new job and new limitations from his injury, he expected to settle into a slower pace of life, maybe even a quiet one. That was until Alice Hart came bulldozing into his world. The woman was anything but quiet. Loud, angry and sexy as hell, yes. But definitely not quiet.

Alice and Brady ignite inside and outside the bedroom. But will they survive the burn?

EXPIRY DATING- the second book in the Bluestone Series is a funny, wild romp along the lines of Stephanie Berget's cowboy romances or Sarina Bowen's True North series. EXPIRY DATING features a retired marine and the feisty young woman who steals his heart. While it is a part of a series, Expiry Dating can be read as a standalone. Grab your copy today.

EXCERPT

There he was—Brady—all six foot two of him. The new bane of her existence. He was wearing a fitted, tan, cop uniform so sexy it should be illegal. If she didn't already know he was the devil, she could easily be fooled by his dark, brooding good looks. Even his damn caramel-coloured eyes were mesmerizing.

Mesmerizing eyes? Get a frigging grip, Alice. He's the devil, remember?

It had been two weeks since they'd met in Vegas at Lily and Jake's impromptu wedding, and despite trying to avoid Brady like the plague since then, he just kept showing up. Yes, Bluestone was small, and Alice was staying at his best friend's ranch, but it was actually getting ridiculous. He was everywhere. Whenever she ventured out, whether it was to get coffee or go shopping, he was there, waiting in the shadows, ready to make her life miserable.

"Looking good, sweetness." Brady smirked as he purposely knocked her on the way over to the fridge, where he swiftly removed a beer bottle.

Alice shot him a glare over her shoulder. "Wish I could say the same to you, Brady, but it appears as if the rumours really are true and beer does go straight to a man's gut."

She was lying, of course. There was no beer belly in sight. The man was a wall of solid muscle, but something about him drove her absolutely insane. It apparently also meant she couldn't control her mouth whenever he was in the vicinity. He'd somehow managed to crawl under her skin in a matter of minutes of them meeting, and insults had been hurled between them ever since.

Brady's silky laughter bellowed behind her. "You offering to help me work it off, sweetness?"

HERO COMPLEX

Fake it till you make it, that's what they say.

And that's what Ivy was doing. She'd do *anything* to save her ranch. Anything. Including pretending to be engaged to a handsome, retired Marine to placate her sexist clients. Not that draping herself over Ace was a hardship. It wasn't. She just wished he could get over his hero complex and stop trying to save her. There were far better ways they could be spending their time.

Sweet, shy, and babbling Ivy had gotten so far under Ace's skin, he knew he was in trouble. Faking a relationship may have been his idea but he knew deep down he didn't stand a chance with her in real life. Medically discharged from the military, it wasn't just internal battle scars he'd been left with, he also had some big ugly ones on his face too. If he couldn't even look himself in the mirror, no one else ever would be able to either. Especially not the most beautiful woman he'd ever laid eyes on.

Can these two wounded souls turn their fake relationship into a real one?

HERO COMPLEX- the third book in the Bluestone Series is a sizzling fake engagement story featuring a scarred Marine and the woman who sees only his big heart. HERO COMPLEX features wide open spaces and ranch life along the lines of Becca Turner's Cowboys of Oklahoma series and D'Ann Lindun's sexy Black Mountain books. While it is a part of a series, HERO COMPLEX can be read as a standalone. Don't miss this captivating and heartfelt romance, pick up your copy today!

EXCERPT:

The sun wasn't even up yet, and Ivy was already having an existential crisis. Even the warm, orange glow from the table lamp did nothing to flatter the reflection staring back at her. One thing was for sure though, no matter how long she looked, nothing was going to change anytime soon.

Internally she berated herself. She didn't have time for this. She had chores to do. Horses to feed. And a sexy-as-hell man to try not to humiliate herself in front of.

"Fucking YouTube." She huffed under her breath before dragging herself away from the tilt of her floor-length mirror.

Damn you, Pricilla28! I'm not feeling sexy OR confident. What a load of crap.

There was no time for Ivy to wallow in the YouTube star's betrayal. Or dwell on her poor judgment at trying out a new hair tutorial at stupid o'clock in the morning. Right now, she had things to do. And that meant leaving the confines of her bedroom with her new hairstyle, which was much more male Viking warrior than the sexy, feminine goddess look she was going for.

Damnit all to hell.

Letting out a heavy sigh, Ivy dragged herself and her manly braid downstairs in search of caffeine. Caffeine wouldn't disappoint her at least. Caffeine was consistent. Reliable. Not at all filled with lies.

With coffee brewed, she was just one sip away from bliss when a loud knock had her cursing again. Back was that funny feeling in her stomach. She knew exactly who was at the door. It had been the same person for the past five days now: Ace. Sweet, kind, thoughtful Ace. Quite possibly the most beautiful man she'd ever seen.

Stop swooning and get it together.

NOW AVAILABLE IN EBOOK AND PRINT WHERE BOOKS ARE SOLD

ACKNOWLEDGEMENTS

I can't thank everyone I've ever met because I'm too old and I'm already at that stage where I'm forgetting names, but really inspiration for my stories have come from all the weird, wonderful, ridiculous, and sometimes painful journeys my life has been made up of. So thank you everyone I've met along the way. Even the rubbish people.

Thank you to Inkspell Publishing for taking a chance on me. In particular I'd like to thank Melissa Keir, owner, editor, fellow author, and badass publisher. Your team of editors and cover designers truly made the Bluestone books a series to be proud of. Inkspell also gave me the opportunity to meet so many talented authors and become involved in a community that not only offered support and encouragement but a safe place to share ideas and experiences.

Finally, you've guessed it, I'm about to thank my family and friends. For putting up with me when I'm grumpy because I've been up all-night writing. For forcing you to read steamy scenes and a whole load of swear words (this one is for my dad, sorry dad!). For not letting me give up. And of course, for believing in me. None of these books would be possible without you.

ABOUT THE AUTHOR

Isobel was born and raised in London. She still lives along the River Thames with her husband and her substantial book collection. Ever the hopeless romantic, she fell in love with the genre from a young age and was inspired to write her own stories. When she's not feasting on romantic comedies or binge reading her hoard of contemporary romance novels, Isobel is writing.

https://www.facebook.com/isobelreedbooks
https://www.instagram.com/isobelreedbooks/
https://www.isobelreed.net/
https://www.amazon.com/author/isobelreed
https://www.goodreads.com/Isobel_Reed
https://www.bookbub.com/authors/isobel-reed

www.ingramcontent.com/pod-product-compliance
Lightning Source LLC
Chambersburg PA
CBHW030342180626
46812CB00007B/2727